THIS IS TRUE LOVE

Stories
and
Essays

Keith Banner

LETHE PRESS

Published in 2020 by Lethe Press.
6 University Drive, Suite 206 / PMB #223 · Amherst, MA 01002
www.lethepressbooks.com · lethepress@aol.com

ISBN: 978-1-59021-709-2 / 1-59021-709-8

Several of the stories in this book are works of fiction. Names, characters, places, and incidents are either products of the author's imagination or areused fictitiously. Any resemblance to actual persons, living or dead, organizations, events, or locales is entirely coincidental.

Set in Electra and Quire Sans Pro
Cover design: Steve Berman
Interior design: Steve Berman

"Hell is a place on earth. Heaven is a place in your head."

-David Wojnarowicz, Close to the Knives

TRUE
LOVE

I've been writing these kinds of stories and essays for thirty years. They are about people, most of them gay, who work shit jobs and have less than wonderful lives. Not that pretty, and a tad-bit sad, they are always trying hard to make it anyway, but usually just shuffled into the background, or scorned when they have the spotlight.

In my mulish allegiance to this endeavor I keep finding reasons to continue it.

Coming up with these stories helps me to know how to love people who often don't end up getting a lot of love. In fact, my focus almost exclusively here is "true love." And for the past twenty-seven years the stories have basically remained the same, except I think I may have gotten to a point here lately where I feel things a little deeper, and am trying harder, as I get old, to figure out how to conjure a fever-pitch empathy and tenderness with the least amount of bull-shit.

Twenty-eight stinking years, here, from the first story I published professionally ("Mars" in *Christopher Street* in 1992) to assorted essays and stories I came across in a plastic tub in my basement I'd totally forgotten about. In that little over a quarter century, by the way, I've published a couple other collections of stories and a novel, but somehow these ones collected here got left out of the mix. They've become my favorites in many ways – full of feeling that year by year has grown into a practice, a habit. The last two stories, written in 2019, are products of all the work before: characters driven by a desire to find a way to love and a way out of their individual predicaments, often stumbling into tragedy, but more often than not finding beautiful yet temporary releases somewhere along the line.

Which is all you can really ask for, in art and in life.

MARS

I was sixteen when Paul was killed.

Paul was Carolyn Carlisle's adopted son. All through my childhood, Carolyn and Paul would come over to our house for dinner, or just to visit. Carolyn, a sweet obese woman with bright red hair, was my mom's best friend from church. She plucked her eyebrows into sharp boomerangs and spoke with a melodic Southern accent. Carolyn and her husband Louie had adopted Paul when he was seven. It was rumored that Paul had been brought up by devil-worshippers before the Carlisles saved him.

Paul was thin, with a stark, mischievous face. He had dark-brown, almost black eyes, and black hair which, in his teens, he chose to wear long, sometimes dyeing it different colors. He had a reputation as a freak at our church, a little Baptist church at the back of a neighborhood near ours. People talked about him all the time. He was the orphan who was sick in the head. Louie had died three years after they'd adopted Paul, a heart attack in the gas station they used to own. Now Carolyn was the single mother of a monster.

Rumors circulated about his being queer, about Paul frequenting the dugouts of abandoned baseball fields after sunset and doing things in the chain-link darkness with other boys and men.

My mom didn't talk about Carolyn or Paul like that. She cared about both of them too much. She was just about the only person who socialized with Carolyn outside of church, and she defended Paul all the time. "He's had a hard life." Or "That's just his way."

It was the early '70s, and Paul was into peace-signs and tie-dyed shirts and Led Zeppelin. He was fourteen and wild. My dad, who didn't attend church, always disliked it when Paul and his mother came over. He didn't know how to respond to Paul, and dreaded having to entertain him. My mom always forced Paul on him, since Paul was fatherless. On Saturday afternoon, he and my father would work together on stilted projects in the back-yard or on the carport. My tall, dark-complected father would be in his work clothes (he wore work clothes even on weekends), and Paul would be in a ripped Army coat and bleached jeans, both of them cleaning Dad's 1972 Impala, or rearranging tools in the tool shed, or pulling weeds. I was a little boy, six years old, and tagged along, helping. I remember thinking of these after-noons as Paul's. I was never that close to my father anyway. But Paul tried to be, at least superficially. He got into their projects, would clean the car and pull weeds excitedly, as if he were acting in a play. Whistling rock songs, Paul would try to make my dad sing along. My dad would laugh sometimes, but mostly he was sulky, wanting to get it over with. Maybe he was a little afraid of Paul. I wasn't.

We lived in a rural area that was only a mile or so from a shopping center, and sometimes Paul and I walked over an over-pass and through a cornfield to get to the K-Mart. My dad didn't want me to go with him, but Mom said it would be fine. She said that it would be okay in front of Carolyn and Paul, to make a point that she wasn't prejudiced against either of them.

"It's just a mile. Just be careful walking cross the road." She gave me a dollar from her tip money to spend.

We would usually hang out at the K-Mart grill, after Paul purchased (or shoplifted) some new hair color, or a Batman comic book, or the new Deep Purple 45. We would drink sui-cides, Paul putting equal amounts of all the fountain sodas into two big cups. In the cool aqua grill, Paul would read me parts of the comic books, or he would tell me how he wanted to build his own motorcycle.

Once, he talked about going out at night. He told me in a whisper, in a fairy-tale voice.

"You promise not to tell?" he said, and he was smiling widely, as if to share in a joke.

"Yeah," I said. I was scared a little by his tone. His eyes got glazed. He leaned forward, across the beige Formica table, elbowing a Spider-man comic book.

"It's great, just to go wandering. At nightcI don't know why I'm telling you this. How old are you?"

"Six," I said.

He laughed.

"Six years old. When I was six I was living with—Jesus—some old lady with a plastic leg. A foster mother. You know what that is?"

"No." I heard a special on bath towels over the p.a. system.

"It's a mother who takes care of you and gets paid for it," he said. "She was great. She'd take off her leg and make a puppet out of it. No, really. She could do that."

I imagined a plastic leg dancing around a living room.

"Anyway. I go out, at night. We're buddies, right? I go out and just walk through neighborhoods. It makes you feel like a king. I mean, not like a king really, as much as someone in control of the outside—Jesus, it's like you own everything outside, at night, you know? You understand?"

I didn't, but I nodded my head.

He was nervous and took out a cigarette.

"Don't tell Mom I smoke. She'd probably have a heart attack."

"Okay."

"What do you dream about?" he asked.

I said I didn't know.

"I dream about water all the time. I mean constantly. Water falling out of a ceiling, water in a doctor's office, me drowning in an ocean. I've never been to the ocean, though. It gets scary sometimes. I don't know. Whatever. When I was four years old, I fell out of a three-story building. Did you know that?"

He dragged off the cigarette, then twirled it in his fingers lovingly. I said I didn't know that.

"I fell out a window. I was just playing around, and then, I don't know, I got this weird feeling that I could float, like I could control myself. Stupid. I remember some old apartment building. I just went out. People thought I was retarded, but no bones broke. That's the weird part. Nothing broke. Forget it."

He started collecting his comic books and cigarettes. He stood up and yawned.

"Let's go," he said.

We walked home.

When he was sixteen, Paul got caught burglarizing somebody's nice house. He was arrested and sent to Plainfield, Indiana, a boy's school there. Carolyn got so emotionally upset that she had to be sedated. But after a while, she got used to it. In church, the preacher would always say during devotions, "And Lord let us pray for Carolyn in her time of trouble." I was eight and interested in what he'd done—what it meant, but no one talked to me about it really, so Paul's disappearance took on the glow of the supernatural. The word "burglary" became exotic, like a magic spell.

By this time, my dad had given up on Paul anyway, and once or twice I'd heard him talk about him with Mom. He called Paul a drug addict and a queer. When he got sent to the boys' school, my dad said, "That's where he belongs." My mom said that no one "belonged" in a boys' school—it just happened.

My mom, Carolyn and I went to visit Paul in boys' school one summer afternoon. Carolyn drove her car, a plush orange Pontiac, to Plainfield, Mom beside her, me in back, excited. When we got there, Carolyn parked beside black wrought-iron gates that said **TO HELP BOYS** in baroque letters. A boys' school officer checked her I.D.

The boys' school looked like a complex of castles, gray stony buildings with slate roofs and sprawling unkempt yards, lots of crusty cement porticoes and water fountains and picnic tables. A few men in uniforms circulated, some positioned in little booths. Long-haired boys in t-shirts smoking cigarettes were everywhere.

For some reason, I kept thinking the boys' school was the Lost City of Atlantis. Mom and Carolyn had dressed up for the occasion: Carolyn in a lavender pleated skirt and white blouse, my mom in one of her best pant outfits. We walked around the buildings, and finally found Paul's dorm. Inside was a fusty, sweaty smell, and the sounds of boys laughing and whistling, toilets flushing, radios blaring. The walls were gray cinder-blocks, with hasty posters detailing movie nights and A.A. meetings. We passed rooms lined with rows of twin beds, shelves above the beds stacked with shaving equipment, comic books, and model cars.

Carolyn spotted Paul by a vending machine near the doors to a gymnasium. He had on a dress-shirt and polyester pants. His hair was between dye-jobs, black at the roots, blonde at the tips. He looked pale and indifferent. He stood by the vending machine with another boy. The boy was in jeans and a white t-shirt with Mickey Mouse on it. He had brown fuzzy hair and strong arms. They were talking to each other intensely.

"Paul honey?" Carolyn asked.

Paul looked up and half-smiled, told the other boy to go away.

"Hey you guys," Paul said to us. His face lit up, but it looked forced.

We walked around the boys' school. At one point, I had to go to the bathroom, and Paul showed me where to go. It was a mint-green, garage-like room, lined with what looked like a hundred urinals. The air smelled raw, like dirty bandages. I heard yelps and laughter coming from behind walls, and I saw two naked boys with towels around their necks coming out of the adjacent showers.

This place was exciting, the way the halls echoed, the way the boys were all grouped together like animals. There was a sexy, frowzy atmosphere everywhere, and even though I was eight, I can remember getting almost sick with it, like eating too much candy. And Paul, at the center of it, always beside me, a tour-guide, pointing out whatever he thought I needed to see.

It was close to dusk, and we were eating candy bars and drinking pop at a picnic table. Paul smoked cigarettes, apologizing every time he lit one.

"It's just something you do here," he said.

My mom asked him what else he did here.

"Well, I go to school till two, and then after two I have like a job, sometimes in the kitchen. Or lawn work. Whatever. It's not that bad."

The sky was turning dark blue, the trees and fencing around the buildings shaking a little in the wind. Lamps along the paths and above the picnic tables began to automatically flicker on.

I saw that Carolyn had tears in her eyes. Paul saw too. He got mad.

"God, Mom. Don't, okay?"

Carolyn nodded, and the tears fell out of her eyes.

"Hey," he said, looking at me, trying to change the subject. "What do you think of this place, huh?"

He smiled, flicking his cigarette to the ground.

I was embarrassed and looked at my mom. She was holding Carolyn's hand with both her hands.

"It's another world, isn't it? It's like Mars," Paul said. He made "Mars" sound musical and funny. He was smiling, but not looking at us anymore.

By the time Paul got out of boys' school, he was old enough to run away. He took off with $250 Carolyn had given him. He called her every-once-in-a-while along the road. Sometimes from New Mexico, New York City, Canada, Florida. My mom gave my father and me reports on him as I grew up: Paul was working at a car-wash in Texas when I was in fifth grade, Paul was digging ditches in Montana when I was in eighth, et cetera. And as I grew up, Paul became a role model, of sorts. He was just about the only person I knew who came close to what I thought I was becoming.

I was gay before I knew what "gay" was. I remember when I was five years old, my father took me to a basketball game he was playing in one November night. He was on a league where he worked. The game took place in an elementary school multi-purpose room. The locker room was locked, so the men had to get dressed for the game on a stage, behind a tall maroon curtain. I went behind the curtain with my father and stood off to the side. The stage was dark, with cardboard trees, and a little plywood fairy tale cabin, leftovers from some school play. Men stripped in the darkness beside the props, peeling off shirts, stepping out of underwear and into jockstraps. They whispered and laughed at each other. Their bodies glowed in the light sifting through the slit in the curtains, and I remember feeling scared but also drawn to the image of bodies stripping in unison, the unselfconscious nudity, the smell of aftershave and sweat. It was a secret pleasure, and I didn't know what I wanted to do, but I knew that the bodies, the secrecy on the stage, the men not knowing what I wanted, all this meant something to me, everything, kind of.

As a kid, growing up, I knew that what I was feeling was "wrong," and I wasn't supposed to recognize what I was doing or becoming. I was supposed to outgrow the urge. My father calling Paul a queer, calling him sick, a Baptist preacher talking about perversion, a grim-faced gay guy on a TV show killing himself because he could not stand what he was—the mystery of what Paul did in the dusky dugouts or in the sweaty stillness of a boys' school—what I myself would eventually do with another boy—all these pointed at rules falling apart. I had nothing to grab onto, to support what I was feeling or what I wanted to do.

Nothing but Paul, an echo of his image coming back and then leaving.

At thirteen, I had sex with another boy from junior high. Brian was his name. It was at a stayover at his house. I lost myself in what we did. We were both pretending to be asleep. Brian was skinny and pale, with dark hair and eyes, and we did it on the floor of his basement. I didn't want it to end.

By the time I was sixteen, I'd had sex with him countless times. We never talked about it or anything. It would ruin it. Every morning, we woke up after doing it and pretended it didn't happen.

One night, in my bedroom, Brian and I were experimenting. I was kissing him, probing his mouth with my tongue. It was three in the morning, and in the middle of the deep kissing, the phone rang. We broke apart instantly.

My mom answered it. It turned out to be Carolyn. She was hysterical.

They had found Paul's mutilated body in a motel room in Fort Lauderdale. I don't know the specifics, just what I heard from

Mom: how Carolyn had to go to the morgue and go through Paul's things, and how the police didn't want to show her the body, but she made them show her the body anyway.

My dad was a pallbearer at the funeral. The service was short, in some bland chapel. I kept thinking as they carried the casket to the front of what was inside. I wondered if the maniac had cut up Paul's face, how many pieces there were, and then this thought grew into what Paul was doing in the motel room.

The preacher did not mention what had happened to Paul's body of course. He said a few words about innocence and children, and then went through a prayer for Carolyn. She sat in front with Mom, sobbing.

After the funeral and the burial, we had a get-together at our house.

The TV was on, without sound. *Adam-12*. Mom had set food out on the table in the small dining room. My dad sat in his chair, drinking a beer, still in his suit. Not many people showed up. Carolyn had stopped crying, but somehow her not crying made me very sad.

After the get-together, I went into the kitchen. Mom was putting stuff into the refrigerator. Just Carolyn, Dad, Mom, and I were here now. Carolyn was lying down, Dad half-asleep in his chair. Mom took Saran Wrap out of its box, biting a section off with her teeth. She looked frantic with the Saran Wrap.

I wanted to say something about Paul, but I didn't know what. The house with dark windows, and Mom putting things away, and Dad and Carolyn sleeping made me feel dislocated. I had no idea why I was here, right now, in this moment.

"What a day," Mom said.

I agreed.

"I think Carolyn's gonna stay all night. Do you mind sleeping out on the couch?"

I said no.

Mom came over to me then. She reached out to me and hugged me real hard.

I couldn't sleep on the couch. I kept seeing Paul's face. I wondered what color his hair was when he had been killed. Mom said he had been a photographer in Florida, taking pictures for a newspaper or something, but that didn't sound true. I saw a motel room in my mind. Once, when I was a little kid, we went to Gatlinburg, Tennessee, on vacation, and stayed in a motel. The clean antiseptic smell came to me, and I envisioned the dark green bedcovers and shag carpeting and paintings of the seashore above the beds and the silvery bathroom. I could hear Paul screaming in the motel room we were in. I could witness his murder. I saw it, but then I pushed it out of my head.

I got up. The house was so dark I wanted to scream. I walked down the hall, and opened the door to my room, and saw Carolyn in my bed: a big bloated woman in a white nightgown, curled up into a ball, softly snoring. I walked toward the bathroom, and heard my parents talking about the whole thing in my head. "I don't know, I just feel sorry for her, Dale, I swear." "It's not her fault. That's just the way he was." "What makes people so crazy?" "I don't know, forget about it, he was a pervert, he was living like an animal—go to sleep."

That weekend, Brian and I camped out in the woods outside of his neighborhood. He had a tent and a lantern and sleeping bags we could take, and we set up camp near the edge of a defunct quarry, played the radio loud. At twilight, we explored the woods. When it got totally dark, we came back to camp and swung a flashlight beam up around tree limbs. It was hot and muggy. We ate Doritos and drank stolen beer and smoked cigarettes sitting outside the little tent. I remember seeing his face in the glow of a flashlight, livid and sharp.

"What a night," he said, and he was smoking another cigarette, holding up his can of beer. It was just something to say. He looked up at the sky. It was marbled in clouds.

"Yeah."

He started talking about seeing some horror movie we'd seen together again. I said yes, sounds good. What a fucking scary flick. But really I was thinking of the woods now. Animal noises. The quarry in front of us, its dark mouth, animals down there.

All of a sudden I started talking about Paul. I told Brian the story of Paul's life. Brian looked uncomfortable.

"And he had to be in closed casket for the service," I said. "Jesus. I keep thinking about when I was a little kid, you know? This is stupid. Everybody said he was queer."

Brian smiled anxiously in the grainy moonlight.

"Man that's terrible. I don't think it was on the news, was it?" He was trying to sound bored.

"No it wasn't, I don't think. Forget it."

We got in our sleeping bags, but it was too hot to sleep in the tent. We went outside, and eventually started fooling around.

I lost interest in most everything after Paul was killed. I got obsessed with him. I thought I was dreaming his dreams: water-dreams, the nightmares inside a boys' school, and the grand finale of severed limbs. I started growing my hair long, listening to the Who, Pink Floyd, Black Sabbath. Paul music. I pierced my ear. My mom and dad got scared of the transformation. I think I began hating them then, all the way.

I wouldn't talk to them about anything. My mom said it was a phase, but my dad was sick of it after a while. He started yelling at me whenever he could. We never really had much of a relationship anyway, so me canceling out what little communication we had drove him crazy inside sometimes. He yelled full-force. Get a haircut. Hit the books. Wear clean clothes. That kind of shit. At times he would try to be sneaky, asking me to go outside to maybe throw the old football around or whatever. Let's go see a movie, huh? But this was strange because he knew I had no interest in doing anything like that with him. I would just look at him, stunned and sarcastic, no matter what he did.

Around that time too, Brian and I started skipping school and getting heavy into what drugs we could find. He'd get pot from his older brother, and there was a guy at school who dealt in homemade speed. We used the dope to accentuate the fucking, although Brian would never admit that we fucked. He mainly used the drugs as an excuse for amnesia: "Man I was so fucked up last night."

We were fucked up in his basement bedroom one night. All the way. It was great. There was a shared fever. I remember we were doing it on the floor, grunting together. In the middle of it, I started thinking about Paul. The room was a motel room suddenly. I thought I saw a knife, a black-gloved hand, sunglasses, a pale face. I remember it was getting close to light outside. Impulsively I screamed Paul's name, and then I looked up and saw someone in the room. I thought it was Carolyn Carlisle for a moment. Big woman in a nightgown, arms crossed.

It turned out to be Brian's divorced mother. She had come down to see what the noise was. We were caught. She freaked out. Her hysteria took the form of organization. She told us to get our clothes on. She said straighten up this room. After calling my parents, she started washing dishes, started throwing things away – old checks and old shoelaces from a drawer in the kitchen, newspapers from beside a chair. She talked to Brian in the kitchen as I waited for my parents at the bottom of the stairs.

"What in the hell were you doing?" his mom asked him.

No response.

"My God, Brian. My God."

He didn't say anything.

"I mean—what in the hell?"

Brian's mom told my father what had happened over the phone. I don't know how she worded it. I remember waiting for him in the foyer, and then seeing him pull up their long driveway in his blue truck. I stepped out the front door. He looked dead. I got in. He did not say anything, pulled out.

At home, I just wanted to go to my room and pack some clothes and leave. I thought this would be the only way to survive. I walked into the house in front of my dad, and my mom was sitting on the couch. She couldn't say anything.

As soon as he came into the house, my dad said, "I don't know what in the hell is going on."

Mom whispered, "Don't."

He was talking to me though.

I didn't know what to say.

"What the hell are you?" he said. He looked at me with tears in his eyes.

I still couldn't talk.

"Why are you doing this to us, huh?" he said. His voice had gone high-pitched.

"Just forget it. Forget it," I said.

My mom sat up, but she didn't come near me. I wondered what she was thinking. Her face was numb. I wondered if she was thinking of Carolyn at the boys' school. I walked into my room.

But I didn't run away. I was too afraid to take the big step. For months, there was incredible tension and ugly looks. I slid into myself, staying in my room most of the time. My parents developed a new attitude, a quiet that relied on humiliation. My father and I stopped pretending we were related. I saw Brian at school, but he avoided even looking at me. I tried to get into schoolwork or whatever, but nothing worked. Quietly stoned, I read books I wasn't supposed to, didn't read the ones assigned, listened to music on headphones. I ended up almost not graduating, second-to-last in my class.

Right after high school, I moved out of the house. I got a job at a restaurant in Indianapolis, and a one-bedroom apartment. I have a few friends at work. I may be promoted to manager in a couple weeks, who knows? I hang out at a couple bars on weekends, or sometimes I don't. Hell, even now, I often think of Paul. Sometimes I want to touch him or wished I had touched him.

Every-once-in-a-while I call my mom.

She's sweet and civil. We've never really discussed what happened that night between Brian and me. We just let that shit go.

Yesterday I called her and she told me nonchalantly: "Your dad and me are getting a divorce. He's moved out."

I kept my mouth shut.

She went on. "You know, you could try going to the community college? It's cheap. They have grants, right? Take a computer class? I don't know. You're really smart. You are. You have to know that. You just need a spark."

"Yeah you're right."

We talked more, but I don't remember the rest.

This I remember:

The day I graduated high school, we had a little party at our house. I didn't really have too many friends at school outside of Brian, so eventually the only person who showed up was Carolyn Carlisle. She dressed in a beautiful mint-green skirt outfit. She looked a lot thinner and paler. Mom hadn't been seeing her as much, and we were all kind of shocked she accepted Mom's invitation and came.

She gave me a card with a ten-dollar bill in it. "To your future," she wrote in red ink on the inside of the card.

We all sat down to dinner that night. Carolyn told us that she'd gone to Paul's grave earlier in the day. She kept looking at her fingernails.

My dad looked over at me then. I don't think I saw hatred in his eyes, or forgiveness, or love. It was an astonished sort of glare, as if he were scanning a lost relative he hadn't seen in years and really never wanted to see again. That glare came and it went, and then he looked down at whatever was on his plate.

"Who's hungry?" Mom said.

WHEN
WE
GO
BACK

Mike watches television without the sound on: a red octopus swirls its tentacles, seeping through black water. It's Tuesday afternoon, and the quiet in the room resembles the quiet in a movie theater before the picture starts, hushed yet with an underlying bubble of whispers, footsteps, and coughs. Mike is in his wheelchair, his legs covered with a blanket. Watching the octopus pour itself into an underwater cage soothes him.

Small shaded lamps make the amber walls glow. Above the brown sofa is a painting of trees. One of the nurses, a black lady with soft eyes, swings by with a tray of pills, says "Hello." Mike just nods; he doesn't want to talk, doesn't want to break his trance.

A commercial comes on, and he flicks off the TV with the remote control. He can feel the pain coming on, a shifting in his body like a tide. Eventually it will focus itself into an ache, sharp and deep, different parts and points of his body. At times, he welcomes the sharpening. When the pain is acute, he has something specific to fight against, to consider out of existence.

There's a smell in the air, an odor from supper, meat cooking, and it sickens him. He can't stop the slide now: the lights swell, nurses pass, the other patients in the hospice cough, talk, wheeze. He stares at a wall clock, an old-fashioned sunburst clock with sword-like sunrays scattering from the clock face. He glares for a minute, trying to witness the pain away, make each sunray a needle of power, collecting them in his brain as the spasm creeps in.

He can hear himself moaning. A cold sweat erupts, and Mike imagines a horizon burning. The pain is immense like that, spreading out inside him like a flat gray sky. He moves his fingers to the joystick, the hum of his wheelchair as he heads for his room, feeling a sear in his pancreas start traveling through his abdomen, a glassy cramp with vibrations. His room doesn't offer comfort. It has a musty familiarity. He closes his eyes tight. His fingers stiffen. He bites the sides of his cheeks. A nurse comes by – a different one, a man, balding in a white pair of pants and a blue sweater. He asks Mike if he's okay. The light flickers on, and the nurse lifts him onto the bed slowly after reconnecting the IV tube, covers him with blankets, turns out the lights.

Sometimes Mike talks to the pain moving inside him, letting it do his thinking for him. Other times, while the pain is sleeping its dull morphine slumber, he has visions of painlessness, his body opened to health, a rediscovery of being alive. It's all imagination, he knows that. Small victories become reasons to stay. The fact that sometimes Mike can pick up an ink pen and write on a notepad is a victory. He writes sentences about staying alive, about what he'll do when he gets better. He knows he is lying but lying or being truthful isn't important—just the fact that he is writing, the blue ink forming word after word slowly in jittery cursive. That's all that matters.

Often he feels victorious looking out the window and seeing the blue sky through orange leaves and being able to imagine Sundays with a lover or with his brother or friends—cold, smoky October Sundays after Danishes and coffee and reading thick newspapers—going outside into the fresh cold, raking leaves, then throwing them up into the air, the wasted, voluptuous feel of piles of leaves and the cold air and touching and laughing and the sun going down as he makes lasagna in his kitchen, or settles into an after-dinner nap.

He holds onto memories that he doesn't know he's actually lived or not. The confusion comforts him though. He spends his days in bed mostly, until the afternoons the nurse comes and helps him into the wheelchair and he can go watch television or write or watch the window. Sometimes they put him on wheeled-in machines or administer suppositories or a psychologist comes and talks about death and he'll listen, but mostly it's just him and he likes it. Likes the solitude. Doesn't want to have to listen to people. People anger him because even though they want to, they can't understand until there are here, where he is. Anger pulses through him and he can barely respond to it outside of allowing it to bloom.

All he knows, at times, is that he wants the freedom of seclusion, so his secrets can ripen. He tends to them when the pain eases up, and he can see bright atmospheres, places to be: a landscape of wide fields with hard winds or afternoons on a warm, salty-aired beach or a delirious astronomy that takes him all the way out of the air. These are places he creates day after day. Places to occupy for minutes or seconds, before the images evaporate, and he's suspended between feeling pain and breathing.

He emerges from a sweaty sleep. His brother Rick is here, dressed in blue jeans and a flannel shirt. His eyes look dark in the yellow-lit room. Mike lies there, looking at him. At first he can't place him, can't find him in his mind.

"Hey—I didn't want to wake you up," Rick says.

"You didn't." His voice feels low and willowy.

Rick says something. Mike looks up.

"Mom and Dad might still come—maybe next week. It's just, it's just so hard for them to take—God, never mind," he says.

The nurse comes in, gives him some pills, and later Rick helps feed him, telling Mike to open his mouth, sliding the warm spoon over his teeth, and the food dissolves into a bitter pablum he can't swallow but he does.

After dinner, they don't talk. Rick sits next to him in a chair. Mike closes his eyes. He can feel him there. He imagines what he looks like through Rick's eyes: skeletal, hair brittle, shabby, too long. He's covered up. Only his head is revealed. He remembers when they were children, and Rick was a little baby and Mike was six or seven—how they shared a room in the old house. When he would get scared at night, he'd get up and carry Rick out of his crib, sleepy and cranky, and would place him in his bed, crawl in with him, sleep next to him in peace.

Rick talks about how his wife is pregnant.

"We found out two days ago," Rick says. "It's weird, I'm gonna be a dad. I don't know."

Mike gets drowsier, and the nausea spatters through his system. He makes himself smile. He sees a world of fetuses stretch out in his mind—an aqua sky of red embryos connected to tubes or tree-roots or something else. The image disappears.

"That's great," he says.

"Yeah," Rick says. "Well you... you better go back to sleep."

Mike wants to say something, but feels unconsciousness coming, a slow dip into a giant fall. Rick dissolves, and Mike flows into his sleep of drugs, the aching almost dull now. Again, he stumbles across that skyful of fetuses, floating soundlessly through air. He feels as if he has been caught up in a drift of other children, a slow tug from his abdomen. The air smells like cold water, and he slips into forgetfulness.

Rick decides to go once Mike has fallen all the way to sleep. The hospice is pretty scary at night. Rick and his wife, Sharon, helped him find the place. Sharon really found it. Her mom is a nurse and gave them a number to call, people to ask. The doctors said it was the best thing: it was more comfortable and intimate here. Mike has gone through a lot of experimental drugs the government now allows. AZT, now DD7 and DDC, protein therapy, chemo. Nothing has worked, although at the hospice they keep giving him AZT and DDC. Mostly, though, he is on painkillers.

It's October. The air is black, with the city glimmering in the distance, a geometric gleam from the skyscrapers, as Rick walks to his truck, hearing the roar of the interstate over on his left. He feels sleepy, and, like always, guilty for leaving. Maybe it has something to do with Mom and Dad. But then he gets rid of that thought, starting up his truck. It's an old Chevy he bought last year, something to drive to work. After a few pumps on the gas, it starts.

He pulls out, gets on the highway. When the symptoms first started getting serious, two years ago, Mike told the family he had AIDs in the kitchen in Mom and Dad's house. They were all sitting at the table after eating, Mike, Rick, Mom, and Dad in this after-supper lull of cigarette smoke and laughter. In the middle of a nothing conversation, Mike just let it come out. Mom and Dad hadn't even known he was gay.

Since then, they'd tried to get over their fears. Mom had even visited Mike when he was in the hospital all those times. She never discussed anything on these stilted visits other than money – how Mike was going to afford all this care. Mom would clutch her purse, smiling awkwardly, Dad's absence haunting each hospital room. About two months ago, when Mike really began looking terrible, going down to 80 or so pounds and the sores gathering on his face, she stopped coming altogether. Now she sends cards and letters, solemn photographs of candles and flowers with small messages scribbled in perfect printing: **WE LOVE YOU**. And Dad helped out on the bills as best he could for a while, like a silent partner, sending the bill collectors hundred-dollar checks. Mike's on Medicaid now anyway.

Rick drives fast, the truck's engine growling, road empty except for a few semis in the opposite lanes. He's afraid for a minute: the fear of getting stuck out in the middle of nowhere. He visits Mike three or four times a week and has developed a way of forgetting his own fears, but still Mike scares him, the emaciated Mike in the hospice room. Rick tries to think of the good times: playing H-O-R-S-E with him, or going to movies when they were kids, Mom dropping them off, or watching Saturday Night Live and smoking dope Mike got at school. As the road flows past him in a dark-silver stream, Rick pictures the sick Mike covered up in blankets, but can also see the other Mike too, the healthy, mouthy one who liked bad jokes and late-night TV and getting drunk as hell. Sometimes, though, this old Mike seems to be a lie, something he uses to make himself happy.

For two months now, Rick has called them before he goes to visit Mike, going over there on weekends, trying to describe for them the situation: "Mike is dying. You have to see him before he dies. You have to." They make promises. Mom does, anyhow. Still when the time comes she always gets scared and declines. It's Dad who sits in his chair, glaring at the TV when Rick mentions Mike. Sometimes Rick can feel the hurt coming from Dad: something in his eyes, a movement that glitters like crying, then evaporates into a numb stare.

Rick decides to go over there tonight. It might be the last chance he has before Mike dies. Besides, he wants to tell Mom and Dad about the baby too. The news about Sharon being pregnant might make it easier for them to go see Mike. He gets off at the next exit, drives over to his parent's place on a secondary road lined with dark trees and broken fences, past Rock Island Refinery, where fiery columns shoot out of smokestacks, blue-white lights flashing onto chain-link fencing and cinderblock buildings.

The house is in an old neighborhood of one-story ranch-styles. Yards and old houses swerve by him in the dark. He pulls into the driveway, and Mom looks out the living room window.

Then she is opening the door, smiling, anxious. He goes in, and Dad is sitting there in his chair watching TV in t-shirt and workpants, his feet in dark socks, his hair fuzzy on top from going bald. The living room is the same as always—exactly how it was when he was little—white walls, dull green furniture, dark wood end and coffee tables. There are old decorations on the walls, gold-painted candleholders and a painting of a wheat field and farmhouse. Mom tells him to have a seat, asks him is he's hungry. She has brownies.

"No thanks."

Dad pushes himself up in the lounger. He turns the TV down with the remote. It's a cop car chasing a pick-up.

Mom sits down on the other side of the couch. She is in her housecoat and footies, her hair combed back into its usual ponytail, her face shiny from Oil of Olay. The room is way too hot. Rick wants to say something mean, something to bring air back into the room.

"It sure is getting cold quicker," Mom says. Her voice almost quivers. They both know why he is here.

"Yeah," Rick says.

"Try working outside in it," Dad says. He works for the gas company, sometimes reading meters, sometimes out on pipeline digs, sometimes in the shop.

"I bet it's lousy," Rick says. He always talks to Dad this way, usually just agreeing, patronizing, and it suddenly angers him, the thought that he contribute to his father's comfortable seclusion.

"Yes, sir," his dad says.

Mom stands up.

"I'm gonna get some brownies. I don't care what you say." She laughs, walks into the kitchen.

Dad looks at Rick.

"Stubborn." Dad laughs.

"Yeah stubborn," Rick says, and it has come out sarcastic and snide. His dad's face loses its calm. His eyes tighten, even squint a little. "Real fucking stubborn."

Mom pokes her head out of the kitchen.

"I saw Mike tonight," Rick says.

They're both silent, not shocked as much as trying to compensate, to get it over with. Rick feels his emotions sharpen, his anger grow.

"I saw Mike, and, um, Jesus—forget it."

Rick stands up, ready to leave.

"How is he?" Mom asks. She stays in the doorway, afraid to enter the room.

Rick laughs. "How is he? Well, Mom, he's about ready to die. That's how he is."

Dad sits up in his chair quietly.

"You're gonna have to see him—you will. I talked to his doctor last week, and he said it's a matter of weeks or days. I mean, I can't believe how you can just keep on ignoring him. This is the last time I'm coming over here begging you guys—the last time, you understand?"

Rick takes a deep breath. Nobody moves. He looks at both of them and feels a sudden opening up, a wave of love for them. They look so old, especially Dad, old and scared and stupid.

"This is so weird. I came to beg you to go see your son, right? And to tell you about me and Sharon. We're having a kid. In the middle of this we're having a baby. Damn."

"You're what?" Mom asks.

"We're having a kid—Sharon and me. In about six months or so. We found out last week."

Mom looks stunned but manages to smile. She comes out of the kitchen doorway and gives Rick an awkward hug, then stands back. Dad stays stooped over in his chair. Rick goes over to him. Dad's face looks stony, untouched by feeling, but then Rick sees a movement in his eyes.

"I'm happy for you," Dad says.

"Yeah," Rick whispers. "God, Dad, you gotta go see Mike. I don't, I mean I'm not saying this to be—I don't know—to scare you, but he's bad. He's.... There's just not enough time to—"

Mom's voice, strained, peculiar, sounds almost like a scream: "We know that."

Dad doesn't say anything.

"You have to go see him."

Dad coughs a little. He gets up slowly out of his chair, turns toward Rick.

Dad whispers, "We' helped out on the bills, and—"

"You need to see him. Both of you. Tell him you love him. I just don't understand why you have to be this way—Jesus Christ..."

Mom wipes her hands on the sides of her housecoat.

"I'm gonna go. I am. Sunday. We can, okay? We'll all go. We will," she says.

Rick gets scared because Dad looks as if he's going to cry.

"Goddammit." Dad's face cracks a little. He rubs his temples, bringing his hands down his cheeks.

"He lied to us, to every last one of us. I don't know who he is. I don't want to know." His voice is low, almost a whisper.

"You just forget everything and go. That's what you do. I mean—do it for me, okay? This may be the last chance. Hell, it is the last chance. I just saw him tonight, and he looks bad. I mean bad. You can't—"

Dad walks out of the room, down the hall, then closes the door to their bedroom. Mom walks past Rick, following Dad, knocks on the door.

"Jack, honey. Let me come in. Come on. Open the door."

The bedroom door swings open. Before she goes in, Mom says, "Call us tomorrow."

Rick says yes, then leaves.

He and Sharon have an apartment in Greenwood, a one bedroom with furniture they bought on credit. Once the baby comes, they're going to try to buy a house somewhere, though Rick doesn't make that much where he works. He does maintenance work at the Greenwood Mall, 200 a week—fixing bathroom fixtures, broken windows, sometimes janitorial stuff. Sharon manages a department at Walmart and makes about the same.

It's close to eleven, and the news is on, quiet when he comes in. Sharon is on the sofa in her oversized nightgown, a make-believe football jersey he got her last Christmas, her dark blonde hair tied back.

He sits down on the couch with her. "I went over to Mom and Dad's after I visited Mike tonight."

Sharon says, "Oh no."

"God. Dad almost lost it. I could see it."

She looks at him seriously.

"So," she asks.

"So Mom said they'd go Sunday. I don't know. This time seemed different I guess. Dad didn't seem as bullheaded you know? I'm not gonna hold my breath though. She's promised that about fifty times before. I'm just hoping, like, when we go back—if—when we go back, all of us together, we'll be able to work something out that's good, you know? I mean not 'good,' just you know, have a chance to be together. You know?"

"Yeah I know.... How's Mike?"

"He was more out of it."

"Did he talk any?"

"Just a few words. Half-asleep conversation."

Sharon guides his head down toward her lap. He lies back.

"I also told Mom and Dad about the baby," he says.

Sharon laughs softly. "God. Having a baby in the middle of all of this. Did you tell Mike about the baby too?"

For her lap, he can smell a clean smell coming from the nightgown—body-heat and Downey mixed together.

"I told him, but I don't know if he understood. He's on a lot of morphine now. Sometimes I wonder if he like shouldn't be back in the hospital maybe or something...."

Sharon says, "It's where he needs to be. He wants to be there, right?"

"I don't think he knows where he is really. I don't know if he even understands who he is."

Rick feels his eyelids come together slowly, the TV light fuzzy, scattering like wings.

Later, at 1:30 in the morning, he gets panicky about not sleeping. He has to be at work at 8:30 to paint. He sits up in bed, and looks at Sharon sleeping, her hair spread across the pillow, her mouth opened slightly. He thinks about the baby, how it will be born after Mike's dead. They weren't trying. It just happened, and they're happy and everything but still he hates thinking about the baby and Mike at the same time.

Sharon stirs in her sleep. She's always liked Mike. One time, all three of them went to a gay bar together to dance, to celebrate Mike's thirtieth birthday, right after he and Sharon had gotten engaged. Rick remembers Sharon and Mike out on the crazy-lit dancefloor, the only male-female couple out there—how beautiful Sharon and Mike looked together, dancing in a frenzy, laughing. He remembers how he was uncomfortable, even queasy, being at that bar—confronted with the oddness of men kissing on each other, and the music brimming over, and Mike, somebody he loved, in the middle of it all that.

Mike told him he was gay ten years ago, way before all this other shit happened. It was Christmas, and they had been staying up drinking Cutty Sark and watching some sci-fi flick at Mom and Dad's house. Halfway through, Mike got serious and the laughter went out of his voice. "I'm tired of lying to you." And he told him. Rick winced at the news, as though Mike had broken some stupid unspoken pact they had. Like they were fucking cowboys or Boy Scouts or something.

For a few months, Rick stayed away from Mike, avoided him, until Mike showed up one night at his apartment, saying, "Jesus Christ, I thought I could fucking trust you. Thanks a lot man— thanks for ignoring me..." And before Mike had turned around to go back to his car, Rick said, "Wait." They'd talked all night. Mike said things like being gay was like being hungry or happy or just alive—it was something he was, that didn't change a goddamn thing. He asked Rick if he should tell Mom and Dad, and Rick, shocked, said they wouldn't understand, so definitely no not now.

Now he bends over and kisses Sharon, whose lips curl, accepting the kiss in her sleep. He lies back down, pushing his feet toward her legs, trying to get comfortable enough to sleep.

Dad comes into his mind then, pictures of him in his chair half-awake watching cop cars, or pulling into the driveway in his gas-company truck. He and Mike and Dad used to go to the Indianapolis 500 in May to watch time trials when they were teenagers. Dad would let them have beers, and all three of them would get drunk and sun-burnt, passing binoculars around—the mean, throaty sound of cars smoking and churning across a black, vibrating track. Mike and Dad really got into it. They'd talk all the way through about A. J. Foyt or Johnny Rutherford, both of them knowing the sponsors of the cars and statistics and world records. Rick remembers the last time they went out to the track together, a blazing May afternoon, a crowded infield, and Mike and Dad laughing together in the heat and exhaust-smells, arm-in-arm on silver bleachers, Mike without a shirt on. It was before even Rick knew Mike was gay, back when there was no struggle and no fear. Before going to sleep, Rick wonders if there's a photograph of that day somewhere.

Sharon and Rick are in the Honda. Rick has on his three-piece suit. He is clutching the steering wheel, watching the road with an intense glare. It's Sunday, and the sky is flabby and everything looks half-awake and raw. Dim trees, the pale buildings, the sloppy houses. It all makes Sharon feel drowsy, each house the same. White aluminum siding and small bald yards.

She has seen Mike several times, and each time the progression is a little scarier. The disease works dark magic, stripping Mike away layer by layer as if it were taking everything—not just her husband's brother's life, but part of her life, too. Maybe all lives.

"I hope they don't chicken out," Rick says.

"If they do, they do. You can't make them go, okay?"

She puts her hand over his hand on the seat, and he licks his lips anxiously. He called his mom yesterday to make sure they were still going. Now he looks at her for a second. "This is so important for Mom and Dad, for me," he says. "They have to come, this is the last chance they'll have I bet. Hell I know."

They pull into Rick's parents' driveway, and his mother pokes her head through the living room curtains, looking terrified.

Rick shuts the car off, and they reach the door just as his mom opens it.

"I'm just about ready," she says, leading them into the living room.

She is wearing a mint-green dress with a white strand of pearls. Her dark hair is done up in stiff curls, and she has on small white earrings, black patent leather shoes. The house smells clean like Lysol and a cake baking.

"Where's Dad?" Rick asks.

His mom turns around on her way down the hall.

"He's not going," she says.

Rick rolls his eyes. "Where the fuck is he?"

His mom looks worried, fidgets with her left earring.

"He's in the bedroom.... Don't bother him. I'm gonna go, though, okay? I'm going for the both of us."

Sharon feels Rick's disappointment bubble over into instant resentment. His face reddens. His eyes intensify.

'What?" Rick's voice goes high-pitched.

His mom pushes in her hair, like she's trying to ignore the whole situation. Sharon doesn't know where to stand, so she just keeps following Rick. His mom looks at her with a desperate, fake-happy face.

"So I hear I'm going to be a grandma."

Sharon smiles. His mom's eyes are scared even though she's trying to be excited, begging for Sharon to say something sweet to her, to ignore Rick's anger.

Rick steps in front of his mother.

"I'm gonna bother him," he says.

Rick's mom closes her eyes slowly. "Don't. Let's just go. Please."

"Fuck it," Rick says. "I'm gonna bother him."

Sharon wants to stop him, but he quickens his pace down the small hallway, pounds on the bedroom door.

"Come on, Rick. Honey, come on. Just leave him alone," Sharon says.

"Dad!"

Sharon goes up to Rick, tries to look into his face.

"Rick—come on, come on now."

Rick stops pounding. He breathes in hot spurts. His eyes won't look at Sharon's. The door stays shut.

"Dad." His voice cracks all the way now. "Dad, come on. Can't you just come on? You're gonna hate yourself, man. When he's gone. You're gonna hate yourself! I can't believe this!"

No sound comes from behind the door. Rick leans against the adjacent wall. His mother comes up behind him, her eyes glazed. She wraps on the door softly.

"Jack?" she says. "Are you okay? Jack?"

Rick wipes his eyes with his hands and Sharon goes to him, holds onto him.

His mother knocks on the door again.

"We're going now Jack. We're going honey," she says.

She stands in front of the door for a minute, as if she's afraid to turn around.

Sharon drives as Rick sits beside her, not saying anything. His mother is in the backseat as quiet as he is. Sharon glimpses back there at her pale face looking lipless, the mouth drawn in, and her eyes gazing blankly at the passing scenery. The silence is frightening, and yet Sharon feels it is an interval of sanity. She remembers their wedding five years ago. Big church affair, how she danced with Rick's dad to big band music, and Rick and Mike and their mother sat at this lacy white table laughing. Rick's mom was proud, smiling at the two of them—her boys, she'd say. Then the three of them got up and she wrapped her arms around their shoulders, and they picked her up off the floor, carried her to where Sharon and their father were dancing. She can remember the whole family like that. Then she thinks that maybe they never really were a family at all. Was if just them acting and showing off?

Her own family fell apart when she was five—a divorce, so she always knew where she stood, knew the truth. Now it seems as if Rick's family is coming apart under the pressure of knowing too much, or maybe just finally knowing, period. Sometimes, even Rick will have a gathering glaze in his eyes when they talk about Mike, not really a hatred of Mike as much as terror of not understanding how to act any more, what to say, what joke to tell, what memory to cling to.

They get off the interstate, travel through several city-blocks. Sharon looks at Rick's mom in the rearview mirror again. She's gazing into her compact, nervously powdering her cheeks and forehead. Sharon thinks about the baby they're going to have. About how love for a kid isn't just being proud of them or happy for them, it's also a fear of what happens to them, fear of what they might become.

They park. They walk toward the big five-story brick building. Rick and his mom look dazed. Sharon watches her hold onto her son's arm, as she walks slowly, her black purse dangling at her side.

Mike is in the wheelchair in the front-room, watching television. He is doped up, but the pain's wide mouth is still opening, murmuring. He is watching a nameless movie about lifeguards. The beach is clean, the sky a blue swell, the tan bodies tight and shiny. He doesn't get the plot, only wants to imagine what it feels like to dive into something cold and soothing and unreal. He sees Rick come into the room. He makes out Sharon too. And behind her he sees his mother, looking scared. He's shocked at first, but then he is hypnotized by their presence. He is able to talk a little.

"What're you watching?" Rick asks.

"I really don't know." He's confused by the question a minute, but then he laughs.

Sharon laughs. She seems real nervous too. Mike remembers the baby.

"I heard about the baby," he says, looking at her. His voice feels liquid. He looks over at his mother, who smiles without showing her teeth like she always does when she's nervous.

"Yeah it's due in six or seven months," Sharon says. "Just call me June Cleaver."

Mike is drowsy, feels extra heavy now. Impulsively he reaches out to his mom. His arms feel as if they are reaching through water, and his mom just stands there for a minute. Then he feels her cold dry fingers in the palms of his hands, and he sees her eyes shut, tears simmering through.

Later, when they go back to his room, he stays in his chair, although Rick and Sharon want to put him to bed. His mom talks about how it's getting colder quicker. They all agree.

"It's not that cold today though," she says.

"Let's go outside," Mike says.

"What? Outside?" Rick sounds shocked.

"Let's go outside. For a minute. Just a minute," Mike says.

Rick just stands in front of him, wide-eyed, disbelieving.

"Do you feel like it? I mean..."

"Yeah."

"Let me go see if it's all right."

Rick walks out into the hall, searching for a nurse. Sharon and Mom just sit there on folding chairs.

"You sure you're up to it?" Sharon asks.

"Yeah I am. Just for a little bit."

Mom doesn't say anything. She looks tiny and panicky, gazing at Mike, then at the door.

Cold air rushes into Mike's face, and he braces himself, breathes it in, his lungs opening in a spasm so that he coughs, tries to ward off coughs. The air is ripe with the smell of dead leaves. Finally, he regulates his breathing, looks out at the scenery. Behind the hospice is a small grass lot and three half-grown trees with orange and yellow leaves, a few parked cars, a chain-link fence. The sky is all clouds. Mike is covered in blankets, weak and nauseated, but the sky and the leaves and the air coming into him are like a medicine for a few moments. His family surrounds him, talking about the weather again, nervous talk that doesn't matter anyway. He listens but doesn't pay any attention. There is forever in the air, a feeling that he can be taken up by it and deposited into a faraway country. But soon the pain snaps right back and it takes over, telling him in a blank thick language who he is and what he is going to be. This is a new pain though, blurred and omniscient, one he doesn't know too well yet. It creeps through his blood and bones like a fog, discoloring the atmosphere, leaving him very aware of where he's at now. He envisions an aerial view, now aware of a new feeling, pure and blunt like the yearning of a child.

ENOCH

The first time I heard a KISS song was with Terry in the attic of his stepmom's house. It was a hot July afternoon, a Saturday. Terry's little cream-colored transistor radio vibrated with "I Wanna Rock 'N Roll All Night and Party Everyday" as we tried to find an old Frisbee. We were bored as hell. The attic smelled musty and raw. Old sweaty furniture sat in shadows, and little holes in the roof let in dusty sunshine. Terry had on shorts and was shirtless, his feet in ragged sweat socks. He was muscular, and his face was lean, with small brown eyes and a pushed-in nose. He'd gotten a perm last week, a loose afro like a nest. Terry's stepmom, a beautician named Lulu, had given him the perm because he said he didn't want to wash and comb his hair all the time. He was busy with his summer job, painting little natural-gas pipe sheds for the gas company. I didn't have a job, but sometimes I hung out with Terry on the job, watching him paint the little buildings that were usually beside railroad tracks. Terry was seventeen, and I was fourteen.

"Look under that couch over there, man," Terry said. His skin was red and peeling, and still had little flecks of white paint on it from yesterday. He lifted a birdcage up off an ornate, broken-down bureau.

"Sure."

I got down on the floor on my stomach. Under the couch were four mousetraps. One had a dry carcass of a mouse in it. The KISS song on the radio made me feel weird, because I'd seen pictures of KISS in a People magazine at the grocery store, and since then I'd always thought they were devil-worshippers. My dad made me listen to gospel music, because he was music director at our church. Dad hated Terry. Terry wasn't a churchgoer. Terry's dad was dead, from a bad liver or some other organ.

I got up.

"Nope," I said.

The tinny rock song continued. Terry went back deep into the attic. Sweat snaked down my face. I was fat and wore a sweatshirt with cut-off sleeves. The sweatshirt helped me hide the flab. I wore shorts and a pair of sneakers. My hair was cut to my skull, Dad's work. Dad had big black electric shears, and every other Saturday night, he would set up a barbershop in the kitchen. As I pulled back a big painting of a dark ocean to look behind it, I thought about how I'd watched Terry's stepmom give him the perm last week. Lulu was thin with dyed blonde hair, and she wore heavy make-up. The perm fluid smelled sickly sweet, like hot poisonous candy. Terry's tall body had been suspended near a yellow tub of water and the dinette table. Lulu's pink-gloved hands massaged the perm fluid in. Terry had talked the whole time about how much time this perm would give him in the mornings.

The KISS song went off. I felt relieved. I saw the KISS faces from People again: one guy had a long tongue, with a white, demonic, clown face, vomiting blood in public. Next was a song by Led Zeppelin, the DJ said. Then the radio went off.

"Fuck," Terry said.

He ran out of the back of the attic to his square little radio, picked it up off the floor, and slammed his hand against one side, but nothing happened.

"I need batteries," he said.

"Yeah," I said.

Terry took the back off the transistor radio, then threw the batteries under the drab sofa, pivoting his arm as if he were throwing dice. He replaced the cover.

"We ain't going to find a Frisbee up here," he said, defeated.

"Yeah," I said.

Terry went over to the couch and sat down on it. He wiped sweat off his forehead. The silence in the attic had bird-chirps in it. Terry just sat there, and I felt queasy, wondering why Terry was even my friend. He was older, and had a job, and yet he hung out with me. Once Mom said that she'd heard Terry wasn't all there, you know, mentally. I thought about Terry's bedroom. He had little Mead notebooks filled with pictures of movie and rock stars, Scotch-taped to notebook paper: Raquel Welch, Burt Reynolds, Elton John, the Bee-Gees. On some of them, Terry had written in careful printing the date and what magazine he had cut them out of and his feelings about each one.

Terry took off his sweat socks and rubbed his toes.

"It's hot up here," he said.

"Yeah," I said.

I moved near the birdcage, near the wall, and started fingering the rusty spokes of the cage. An old bird smell came out of there, raw ammonia, the dustiness of feathers. Terry pulled back his curly hair, slouching on the sofa. I looked at Terry's radio beside his thigh. Again, I could hear the echo of KISS. I saw them: black-leather costumes and painted-up faces, long hair, spike heels, electric guitars. My dad played George Beverly Shea and Tennessee Ernie Ford singing "Amazing Grace," "I've Found the Light," "Just as I Am," and other tunes at night. I remembered last summer, when I hadn't known Terry. How I'd won a contest for memorizing the most Bible verses at Vacation Bible School: 37. Dad, who'd run VBS, had crowned me with a construction paper crown with glitter on it at a night-convocation in church. I'd also won a huge Hershey bar, which I ate that night in my bedroom. One of those memorized Bible verses bloomed in my head then: "And Enoch walked with God: and he was not, for God took him. Genesis 5, verse 24."

Terry slipped off his shorts. Terry sat there.

"No Frisbee today," he said.

He was hard, and he started doing it to himself. I watched, and my cheeks got hot until they felt hard, like baked potatoes. I was smiling, but it was a mask. Terry looked scary and beautiful, with his face opening as he did it. There was a slight sucking sound from what he was doing. I pulled down my shorts. Terry moaned. I stood near the birdcage with my underwear still on, watching him, and suddenly I wanted to cry. I thought I could smell Terry's loneliness as I watched him jack off. It was the smell of old furniture and rotten wood, those dusty feathers. But the sadness only mingled with my own heat and desire. I hated Terry for a second, but even that went away. Mostly I was impressed. The heat got intense, like radiation. I pulled down my underwear, keeping my shirt on. Terry rose off the couch, making an arc with his body, his head pressed against the back of the sofa. His head went back and forth as he did it.

It was like, for a second, I could not breathe anymore. I was caught up in a breathless little fury. The birdcage fell off onto the floor, making a sound like someone pounding on a piano, but neither of us were going to stop.

GOODBYE
SCOTT

Trent sat down at the dinette table and unfolded the note that had been taped to his door, staring at it:

Get those blankets off the windows! You have to have *curtains*. You boys know the rules. This is your last warning. The *management*.

"The management" was a short, stocky old guy who had head problems. He lived in the apartment at the front of the complex. Now that Scott, his roommate, was going, Trent felt like he had no way to escape the exclamation marks of a fucked-up landlord. He took off his chef's hat, twirled it, then folded it, thinking of how Scott would handle the note. Wad it up and throw it in the corner, forget about it until the next one arrived. Scott's stuff, mostly t-shirts, music cassettes, and shoes, was packed haphazardly in milk crates, sitting under the army-blanketed windows. Trent went over and rearranged some of the shoes. Scott's buddy in Houston had gotten him a job in construction there. Tomorrow, Trent would be taking Scott to the bus depot, and that would be the end of it.

After taking a shower, Trent stood naked in front of the mirror on the back of the bedroom door. He and Scott shared a room, two lumpy twin beds like a barracks, pushed against adjacent walls. The beds used to be bunkbeds, from when Trent was a kid. Their moving in together had been Trent's idea. They both worked at Steak-N-Shake, Trent a cook, Scott a dishwasher who wouldn't have ever got moved out of the dish room because he was always goofing off, spraying people with the dish-machine hose, never taking out the trash when he was told to by the manager until the garbage piled up in back at the end of the night like a landfill. Two months back, Scott had been kicked out of his place, and Trent had wanted to help him out. It was his apartment, and he could swing the rent for the both of them, he had told Scott. No big deal. Still there had been the other reason Trent had wanted Scott here, a wish that, like an accident, Scott would end up in Trent's bed, silent and open-eyed, as Trent kissed him on the mouth and held him and all the other things.

Trent studied himself in the full-length mirror. His dark hair was cut short, his body skinny and pale. He felt disconnected from the image right then, as if he were watching a movie in which someone was looking at himself. Trent went over to Scott's unmade bed, lay in it for a minute, closing his eyes, smelling Scott's dried-out, sweaty odor in the sheets. As he jerked off, Trent couldn't push his mind away from the fact that what he was doing was making things worse for himself. He was torturing himself, he knew this, but he did not want to stop.

The curtains Trent found at the Salvation Army were bright yellow and wrinkled, but he knew they would fit. When he came home with the stuff, Scott had the stereo turned up too loud, and Trent remembered a run-in they'd had with the landlord when Scott first moved in. There had been a pounding on the door, and Scott answered. "Turn that fucking music down!" the landlord had said, standing on the concrete porch. Scott, a little shocked but able to play it cool, said, "What music? I don't hear any music. Do you hear anything Trent?" Trent smiled, wanting to play along, but seeing the landlord out on the porch, he buckled under and went to the boombox, turned the volume down, and then told the landlord to chill out.

Now Trent put the curtains on the dinette-table, pulling the old blankets down from the windows and folding them.

"Hey," Scott said, carrying a pile of clothes from the bedroom to his crates. He was in a pair of cut-off jeans and no shirt or shoes. His blonde hair was messy from not being combed.

"Hey," Trent said.

"I saw that fucking note on the table. Man, that landlord guy is a total screwhead."

"I know."

Scott looked over at the curtains on the table. "Did you buy curtains?"

"Yeah."

"Jesus," Scott said. His voice sounded pompous. "I guess you had no choice."

Scott was judging him for buying goddamned curtains. Just because he was going to Houston, he was the big outlaw. Trent didn't say anything, too ashamed to put the curtains up now. He went and turned the stereo down, while Scott stuffed his jeans in with the cassettes and shoes in the crates. Scott looked up at him. "So you don't mind taking me to the bus station tomorrow?"

"Naw."

Scott went into the bedroom and came back out with a pair of old aluminum crutches he kept around just in case he needed them because of a trick knee. Pretending to be crippled, Scott stood in the middle of the room on them, not saying anything about what he was doing.

"Yeah, I'm gonna miss this place."

Scott smiled. "Not," he said. He laughed, throwing the crutches down, walked around like a little kid just learning to walk. He did an impersonation of a televangelist: "Healed! I am heeee-aled."

Trent laughed, and then suddenly he wanted to cry.

Scott, seeing Trent's change of emotions, picked up one of the crutches and played a little air-guitar with it, being real stupid about it.

"Yep. I'm gonna miss this," he said, laughing.

Trent woke with a start. It was still dark out, only 5:30. He looked over at Scott, who was sleeping without his shirt on, his mouth opened wide, his hair spread out as if he were falling. Trent noticed the indentation of Scott's chest at the center, how the muscle seemed to sweep out from a bone in the middle like petals on a flower. He thought about all the times he stared at Scott like this, wishing his stare would somehow enter into Scott's dreams like a laser, burning into Scott's sleep until Scott would wake up a changed person, and the two of them would be in love at the same time. Trent sat up in his bed. He had tried very hard, since he'd started feeling this way, to stifle all of it, and it usually worked. Splitting himself in two, he would go all ghost-like and be able to forget what he was thinking most of the time. Now, though, with Scott leaving, he felt himself somehow coming back together.

Quietly, careful not to wake Scott, Trent got dressed, drove to a convenience store, and got some donuts, juice, two giant cups of coffee, a pack of cigarettes, and a new lighter. On the way back, he passed the Steak-N-Shake, where he worked and Scott used to work. The sign was lit up a fluorescent white in the cold, dark morning. Last week, Trent had put up the message on the western side of the sign: **GOODBYE SCOTT**. They did this any-time anyone left who'd work there for a while. He remembered doing it as a lesson to himself, volunteering during a slow period to go out and get it done (usually the maintenance guy did the sign, but he had gone home sick), each big black letter a way to realize that Scott was nothing to him. With the long aluminum rod with a suction cup at the end, he had centered the message, a cold wind blowing into his face. Gradually, as the message was organized on the large board, Trent began to feel grateful Scott was going. After Scott left, then maybe he could get on with his life. Trent had had girlfriends before, nice ones, a waitress at

Steak-N-Shake, one girl he met when he had gone to church that one time. As he drove back this morning, the message seemed almost anonymous, a **SCOTT** in all caps he did not know. Inside the restaurant he saw people eating and working.

When he got back, Trent put all the stuff on the dinette-table, scooting the sack of curtains over. He arranged the boxes of donuts, the large cups of coffee, and the container of orange juice on the table, put the cigarettes and new lighter in his pocket. Trent had made chili or spaghetti some nights, and Scott and he would eat together, then sit around watching TV, Trent secretly feeling a satisfaction, well-fed and looking at Scott's face in the dark.

Trent opened the box of donuts carefully. It hit him that since he was thirteen, for almost ten years, he had been waiting for this shit to stop and start over, like a cassette-tape. His mom, who lived fifty miles north in Muncie, kept calling him and hinting about girlfriends, et cetera. She and his dad had gotten married when they were nineteen, and now both of them were wondering when he would settle down. Every time she called, Trent told her he was dating a different name. Last Thanksgiving, when Scott had just moved in with him, they had gone over to Trent's house to eat. Their house, the one he had grown up in, was small, a whitewashed tract house near the factory where Dad worked. Scott ate a lot, and Mom and Dad had liked him, as if Scott were their real son, and Trent were Scott's goofy sidekick. Mom made remarks about Scott's good skin, and Dad asked Scott if he had played football in high school, which he had but he said he wasn't any good at it and laughed.

"Boy," Dad said. "I tried to get this one to even try out. No way." Flabby in corduroy pants and a plaid shirt, his hair greased back, Dad sat in his recliner like a person in a wheelchair.

Nobody said anything to that. Trent had tried out a few times, but his heart hadn't been in it. Trent sat there, a little humiliated, and yet glad Scott was there. Scott was someone Trent had brought home, tan and handsome, his friend; he was kind of showing Scott off the way a newlywed shows off his wife, with pride and respect, a sense of accomplishment. But it was also was a big joke on everyone.

Mom doled out pieces of pumpkin pie with whipped topping.

"Eat up," she said.

Trent heard Scott's alarm clock now, and he went into the bedroom. Scott was sleeping through the alarm, so Trent stepped over and flicked it off. Still Scott slept.

"Scott?"

He didn't respond.

"Hey, Scott?"

Trent bent down and shook Scott's shoulder. He slowly opened his eyes.

"I got some breakfast," Trent said.

The two of them went into the living room. It was still dawn-dark.

"Hey man, this looks great," Scott said, his voice hoarse.

They sat at the dinette-table and ate quietly. Trent could barely swallow the food. Scott shoved a donut into his mouth, still half-asleep.

"Thanks for the breakfast," Scott smiled, then sat up and walked into the bathroom to take his shower.

Trent stayed out in the living room until he was sure Scott was under the water. He walked toward the bathroom door and stood there. Steam started pulsing out, and Trent could hear the water hissing. He smelled the soap and the heat, going back to Scott's bed and lying on it, unzipping his pants. He smelled

Scott's smell again, mixing in with the moist, soap steam. He buried his head in the sheets, then turned back over and jerked off, listening to Scott's shower, hoping that Scott might catch him, until finally he came, as Scott shut off the water. He sat up and walked into the living room, the windows lighting up with dawn, cleaning himself with paper-towels in the small kitchen in the dark because the kitchen had no window and he did not want to turn on a light.

Through the walls, he heard Scott turn the boombox on again. Trent threw the towels away, and felt peaceful, standing above the trash can. All this would go away, he thought. Then he remembered a guy from down the block named Kevin he'd jerked off with in the ninth and tenth grade, the guy who had moved away when they were to be Juniors. He remembered this same intense feeling being snuffed off, like a heel on a match-stick, then his life continuing like anybody else's. Somehow, though, this time felt different. He was older and saying goodbye, not a kid anymore knowing that eventually he would be right in the head. The difference seemed like the difference between knowing who you were and knowing who somebody else was. It was okay for somebody else to feel this way, even the act on it, but for him it was like separating from his own skin, turning away from his own bones.

Scott was standing in the doorway, drying his hair.

"Why are you standing in here in the dark?"

Trent shrugged his shoulders.

"You about ready to go?"

Trent said sure.

The bus station was a long corridor with a bay of greasy windows. The buses waited like missiles. Only people with tickets and their guests could get into where the seats were.

Scott had on a leather coat and jeans and boots and his Nike t-shirt. He had one suitcase. They sat for a little while on hard plastic seats.

"Yeah. My mom'll come and get the shit at the apartment next week sometime. She's gonna store it for me. Cool?"

Trent said yes. He got up. Scott did too.

"I gotta get to work," Trent said.

Scott stood there.

"Well, man, I'll send you a postcard."

They shook hands.

"Yeah," Trent said, but he was pissed suddenly. He stood there.

Scott sat back down and looked up at him. "Yeah?" he said.

Trent didn't know what he wanted to do, but then it hit him.

"You know," he said. Scott was slouching in his chair. "Um. Like you live with me, for what? Two months. And I paid the rent all that time."

Trent's mouth went dry, and his voice felt like fingernails scratching at his throat.

Scott sat up, his eyes slit. "Yeah, but that was your fucking idea."

"I know."

Scott started laughing. "So? I mean, all the money I have I spent on this ticket."

"I know that."

The bus station echoed with a garbled PA voice.

"I just thought maybe you'd want to say thanks or something," Trent said.

Scott's face went solemn then. For one moment, it was like maybe Scott cared, or maybe it was like he understood how

Trent cared about him. Either way, Trent felt ashamed. It was too much. Scott's voice went low and sincere.

"I've thanked you. Hell I have. I mean I thought I had. Sorry, man. Thanks. Yeah. Thank you. Thank. You. Okay?"

Trent smiled. He felt he had to. Scott was looking at him.

"That was all I wanted," he said, but he could not step away, could not just let it die. He knew he should, that what he had just said was the end of what they had together, but he could not pull himself away from the scene.

"What?" Scott asked, and he was scared you could tell.

Trent stood there and wished he could leave.

"What's wrong?"

Trent bit his bottom lip very hard, then licked the indentations his teeth had made.

Scott got up and stepped close to him. "What is wrong with you?"

"I love you," Trent said. "Don't go."

Saying it felt as if the whole world had come to a stop, a standstill in his heart. He looked at Scott, and Scott was looking down at the floor.

"Fuck," Scott whispered.

Trent wanted to run, but he stood there and tried to smile, and he didn't know why he was standing there trying to fucking smile. He looked out at the buses waiting to leave.

The sun was coming through the naked windows. Trent was groggy. It was Monday morning, and the yellow curtains he'd bought at the Salvation Army were still sitting on the table in their white plastic bag. He'd worked doubles both Saturday and Sunday. Now he felt watched. He got a cup of instant coffee and sat down on the couch in his underwear, looking out at the parking lot. As he looked at all the sloppily-packed crap, still sitting under the windows, he got the urge to burn it all. He heard someone tapping at the door but didn't answer it. The tapping turned into pounding, but Trent didn't move.

"Hey! Hey!" It was the landlord's voice. "You in there?"

Trent got up and went to the door but he didn't open it.

"Yeah what?" he said.

"I left you that note Friday, and now there aren't any curtains up. What is this? You boys know the rules."

"Why don't you just leave me the fuck alone?" Trent said. "I bought curtains Friday night, and I'll put them up when I am good and goddamned ready."

Trent opened the door then. The landlord, short, stocky, and pale in green overalls, stood there with his face knotted up. He had a crew-cut and it glittered like the bristle on a metal brush. Trent stepped up to him and felt powerful all of a sudden.

"Leave me the fuck alone," he whispered.

The landlord stared at him in shock. "I'll have you ass evicted buddy."

"Go ahead."

The landlord didn't say anything more.

Trent slammed the door, then heard the landlord's footsteps. He saw that stocky fucker walk back to his office, thinking of what he might be thinking: two guys living together in a one-bedroom. That was why the landlord was all over them all the time, bitching like that over little things to get them both to leave. Scott had already left, though. Trent imagined himself going to the landlord's apartment and pounding on the door and beating the shit out of him, but he knew he couldn't do that, he didn't have that in him. The anger was there, though, pure and gassy like a propane torch. He sat down on the couch, and began to think about Scott again, Saturday morning, Scott staring at him after he'd told him he loved him in the bus station like that.

Scott had grabbed hold of his duffel bag angrily after a voice on the PA system called out his departure. He was getting ready to walk away, but he stood in front of him for a few seconds. Trent was wiping at his own face angrily.

"Listen," Scott said. "I didn't know you felt like that. I mean, maybe I knew but just, you know, I had to have some place to fucking live until Houston came through, so I let it go. Right now, I'd like to beat the living shit out of you, but I don't know. I feel sorry for you to be honest. I'm out of here. Get some therapy."

"Go to hell," Trent said, his knees wobbly. His shame had turned itself into anger as Scott stood there, and the transformation, at least for a few seconds, was pleasurable and breath-taking.

"Right," Scott said.

Trent watched Scott get onto the bus. The bus took off, hissing, with the fish faces of passengers passing by in smoke-colored windows, disappearing down the street.

That night, Trent took the sign down at work. The black letters were frozen onto the fluorescent backing. He had a hell of a time. When he got to **SCOTT**, he stopped for a minute. That was all that was on the sign, below the Steak-N-Shake logo: **SCOTT**, in the center. In the cold, he pictured Scott's body, Scott's small red mouth and blonde hair. His own body was filled with an unbelievable warmth and tenderness, despite everything. He stared up at that name. He knew it would only be a short time before he would have to find someone else to love like that, all-encompassing and thoughtless, like his blood was causing it all. And the next time, somehow, this guy would have to love him back, no matter what. This new stubbornness, this fearlessness, thrilled him for a moment, overtook everything. It would have to happen, Trent knew, or he would die.

**MONKEYBOY
FLIES
THROUGH
THE
NIGHT**

On his break, Asa walked over to the Dairy Queen across from the gas station where he worked. He took the piece of cardboard he had been drawing on with him, got a cup of coffee, and sat in a booth in back. Immediately he started working on his picture some more, a drawing of Marilyn Monroe from memory, in a flowing skirt. He had drawn her so many times that this was second nature to him.

There was a strange man who worked at the Dairy Queen, a thin man with a five o'clock shadow in a yellow smock, with small wet eyes. His name-tag said "Jerry." Now Jerry swept near Asa, and Asa felt self-conscious, but continued to draw anyway. Jerry came over to him as he swept and eventually started laughing. He dropped his broom on the floor, the stick making a startling slap.

"That is beautiful!" Jerry said, pointing at the drawing. His voice was effeminate and hillbilly.

Asa looked up. "Thanks."

"You can really draw. It looks just like her."

"Thanks."

Jerry bent down and picked up his broom.

"You work over at the Phillips 66? You're a good artist my friend."

"Yeah." Asa folded the drawing and put it into his overall pocket. He stood up. "I go to art school in Indianapolis at night, part-time."

Jerry followed Asa to the trash bin.

"You think you could draw me something? I mean, for money? How much do you charge?"

Jerry's eyes glinted sincerely, and Asa felt obligated to him.

"Oh I don't know."

"Well listen, I'll pay you twenty-five dollars if you draw me a picture of this photograph I have, okay?"

"Sure," Asa said.

They walked toward the front doors, Jerry putting the broom up against the cash register. "I'll bring the picture over to the gas station. When do you get off?"

"One."

"Good. I'm off at eleven. I only work part-time because my mom's so sick."

Asa smiled at Jerry, and Jerry smiled back. Asa noticed a delirious kindness in Jerry's smile, a helplessness too.

"I'll bring it over at one then," Jerry said, and he walked outside with Asa.

"I'll see you," Asa said, scared and walking backwards.

Jerry waved, then disappeared into the Dairy Queen.

Sometimes as Asa pushed the nozzle into the tank, he would look over at the Dairy Queen sign. He had seen Jerry yesterday put up the message on the marquee: **HAVE A GOOLISH HOLIDAY**. Asa wondered if Jerry had something wrong with him, mental-wise. Asa had a cousin who lived in an institution years ago. He had a small, monkey-shaped head and could not talk, only growl. Monkeyboy, Asa thought, giving the lady in the cream-colored Cadillac her change. Monkeyboy caused his mother, Asa's mom's sister, to go insane, they all said. Monkeyboy's father left then, and Monkeyboy's mother started acting like Monkeyboy didn't exist anymore, stopped visiting him, until it was only Asa's mom who went to the institution out on the interstate toward Terre Haute. She would come back and tell them about Ansel, which was Monkeyboy's name: how Ansel had scratched on his chin until it made a bloody place, how Ansel had pooped his pants, how Ansel played with himself in the lounge in front of everyone. One day, though, Ansel got sent to another institution in Pennsylvania, and then no one had to talk about him anymore.

At one o'clock on the dot, Jerry showed up on a bicycle. He had changed from the Dairy Queen uniform shirt into a pair of jeans and a flannel shirt. He looked like a little kid. It was chilly, so the two of them got into Asa's car.

"I hate working at Dairy Queen," Jerry said, fiddling with the broken window-roller on the door.

"I hate the gas station just as much, I bet," said Asa.

"Yeah, but at least you go to school. You have a future."

"I guess."

Jerry pulled a manila envelope from his back pocket. He gave it to Asa without saying anything. Inside was twenty-dollar and a five-dollar bill. There was also a picture from a dirty magazine of a naked man standing outside a shower-stall. His flesh was tan and wet, and he had black shiny hair and a mustache, with an orange towel handing around his neck. His penis was long and hard, and he was smiling as a father might smile, strong but forgiving.

Asa looked at the picture. He did not know what to say.

"Is twenty-five enough?" Jerry's face was pale, his mouth drawn in. It was almost as if he were going to cry.

"Yes," Asa said. "That's enough."

"Good."

They sat in the car for a minute or two, as Asa put the picture back into the envelope.

"Well, I'll see you tomorrow maybe," Jerry said. He got out of the car. Asa watched him get on his bike. The trees around the back of the gas station were bright orange, the sky cold and blue. Jerry pedaled away furiously.

Asa drew the picture in his bedroom. As time passed, Asa fell into a trance, drawing the anonymous man's genitalia, his eyes, his mouth. He thought as he drew about the one and only time he went to see Monkeyboy with his mother, in the gray-green institutional dayroom. Monkeyboy had on dirty pajamas. He played with himself in front of everyone, but no one said anything. Asa remembered feeling close to Ansel, standing in his damp raincoat watching Ansel give himself pleasure until one of the orderlies swatted his hands, Asa's mother whispering, "About time they did something."

The orderlies put Ansel's hands behind his back with yellow vinyl restraints. Ansel's mom was the one who had coined the term "Monkeyboy," but never in front of Ansel's mom, just other family. Ansel sat on the floor, rocking back and forth, sometimes hitting the base of a floor-lamp. His face was too small for his body, his dark hair shaved to the scalp, his lips chapped raw.

Mom, who was skinny then, in a rain bonnet, talked to Ansel. "Why do you do this every time I come to see you?"

Ansel did not answer, only growled.

Mom looked at Asa. He was standing near the corner now, afraid.

"Look at that," she said to Asa.

Ansel rocked. The orderlies were at the front-desk now, keeping an eye on him. Ansel's growls escalated to screams. Asa stayed by the corner. Mom bent down and Ansel screamed louder.

"Just forget your present," she said to Ansel, running away.

Ansel stood up then. He was screaming, but in a split second he stopped, as if someone had flicked a switch. With his hands behind his back, he just stood there; then he began to hum a song, "Row row row your boat." The melody was frightening and almost perfect.

Mom went over to Asa and grabbed his hand. They walked out to the car, Mom explaining, "It's just pitiful."

After art class one night, Asa went with Eddie and Doug, two fellow students, to their apartment for coffee, but the coffee never got made. Eddie and Doug, full-time students, sat on a beanbag chair together on the dusty wood floor, laughing and smoking a joint while Asa sat on the lumpy sofa, watching them. They started to kiss eventually.

"He likes to watch," Eddie said.

Asa felt shocked that he was being noticed.

"What?" he asked.

"I said," Eddie stood from the beanbag, pushing back his long and ratty hair, "that you like to watch."

Asa sat there. "I guess so." He didn't mean to say that. He felt the top of his head, the bristles of the flat top which he went to the barber every other Friday morning to have shaved.

"Come here," Eddie said, and Asa stood up.

Eddie laughed, looking at Doug. "Isn't he a winner?"

Doug didn't say anything. Doug had a goatee and wore a ripped painted-smudged flannel shirt, lighting a cigarette thoughtfully.

As Asa approached Eddie, he pictured the man in the photo Jerry had given him. The portrait he was drawing was half done, and it was not very good. Still the man haunted Asa, frozen in Asa's mind into that awkward, after-shower pornographic/masculine attitude.

Eddie smelled of burned weeds and body odor. He had plaid pants and a paint-smudged t-shirt on, his eyes smeared with mascara. At that moment, feeling patronized and stupid, Asa did not want to be kissed, and yet Eddie kissed him and he stood there and accepted it.

Asa walked back from the kiss as soon as it was over, almost hitting the wall.

"I thought you two were married," he said, trying to be funny.

"No," Eddie said. "We're just friends. We don't even fuck most of the time."

"Yeah," Doug said angrily. "We're evil and promiscuous, Asa."

Doug laughed again, but his laugh sounded hurt, as if he did not want Eddie kissing other people. He stood up and went to the bathroom, slamming the door.

Eddie flopped down on the beanbag. He looked pleased and tired. "You're a good kisser," Eddie said. "You kiss like a love-starved freak."

Asa looked down at his shoes.

"I gotta go."

He walked out without saying goodbye.

Asa had not been to his part-time art class for two weeks, since that night at Eddie and Doug's. He took time off to finish Jerry's drawing. Now that it was finished, Asa was not proud of it. It was just a picture of a naked man, out of proportion. The man's head was too big. His fingers were raw-looking from erasing. Asa always had trouble with fingers. He took the drawing to Jerry on his coffee break, the third week of November, and Jerry loved it.

"This is really great," he said. "God, you are amazing. It looks great. I am definitely going to frame it."

Asa realized that Jerry had the same expression on his face Ansel often did, a lost and hungry grin below crazy and joyful eyes. Sometimes he noticed that expression on his own face and would stand in front of the mirror, mesmerized by it, but also terrified because he had not intended on making it.

Jerry said, "Would you like to come over some time and eat with us?"

"Us?" Asa asked.

"Me and my mom. You know. She's sick. There's a nurse that comes in, but basically I take care of her. She is out of her head sick. Not the nurse. My mom. She says all kinds of stuff and keeps forgetting her own name. God, this picture. It's something to live for."

Jerry gave Asa a knowing glance, the glance of someone sharing a deep secret, and at that moment Asa felt scared and wanted to take the picture away from Jerry and rip it to shreds, but then he knew this impulse would only be replaced by the desire to get down on his knees and pick up each shred and Scotch-tape it back together.

Jerry hid the picture as his manager passed.

"Listen, I have to go," he said.

"Yeah."

"Really. I want you to come to dinner. By seven or so, Mom's sleeping, thank God."

Asa looked over at a banana-split sign in the window, dusty and hung at an awkward angle.

"I don't know," he said.

"Tomorrow?"

Jerry was holding the picture in a scroll, looking at him with impatient eyes.

"Sure," Asa said.

Asa's obese mother sat at the kitchen table, cleaning out her purse. Dad was in the adjacent den, watching a rerun.

"Here," Asa said. He gave her the envelope with his rent in it.

His mom took it and put it aside.

"Aren't you going to count it?" he said a little hatefully. Although they said it was only because Asa was an adult now, Asa knew his parents were making him pay rent for his own room because he had stopped going to church with them. They felt betrayed. But he was nineteen and it was time to get on with his life.

"I trust you," she said, not looking up.

Dad said, "Here, let me count it." Skinny and bald, he had stood up and was now lighting a cigarette at the kitchen table. He opened the envelope and took the money out, and his father said in a smart-aleck tone, "It's all there. You're a fine, upstanding citizen."

Asa went into his room. His room had not changed in six years. The pictures on the walls were drawings he had done in high school of Marilyn Monroe, a bowl of fruit, a field with trees, and James Dean. He had won a second-place ribbon in an art-show for the Marilyn drawing; it was done in colored pencil, Marilyn's flesh pink and shiny. Asa remembered the days and night he had worked on it in this room his sophomore year. Now the room's sameness made him feel safe but slightly unstable, about to fall off a cliff and yet also aware that there was no other choice.

He dressed in his best clothes and began to feel a headache as he tied his necktie.

Mom said, as Asa was about to leave, "Where are you off to now?"

"A date."

Mom came out of the kitchen, looking totally shocked and pleased in her yellow housecoat, "Who?"

"None of your business," he said.

Mom laughed, "Is she one of those hot ones?"

"Yes," he said.

Mom came over to him and straightened his necktie. "It's about time you got out and dated. We were really worried, but we didn't say anything."

His dad came in then. Mom turned around. "He's got a date."

Dad grinned. "What's her name?"

"For me to know and for you to kind out," Asa said.

Dad opened the envelope with the rent in it and took out a twenty-dollar bill. "Well, whatever her name is, smarty-pants, go buy her some flowers. I think they still do stuff like that, don't they?"

He was asking Mom. She pretended to slap him.

"Yes they do, dummy. You ought to try it." Mom got serious, looking at Asa. "Does she go to church?"

"I don't know."

"If she goes to church, that'll do you good, too. Really, son, what is her name?"

Mom and Dad stood beside each other. They were holding hands, rejuvenated. Asa looked at them without saying anything else, feeling as if he were seeing through them into an abyss. He smiled like it was a little game he was playing, keeping the name a secret. He thought how simple they must think things are. In a strange burst of love, he pitied them, and suddenly wanted to kill both of them, smother them during the night with a pillow, in order to save them from themselves. He backed up toward the door.

"Well, have a good one," Mom said. "Tell that little whoever I want to meet her ASAP."

"Don't do anything I wouldn't do," Dad winked.

As he walked up the street toward Jerry's house, Asa thought about Monkeyboy again. In his mind, Monkeyboy had become more attractive, sexy in a renegade, Eddie-like way, and he imagined Monkeyboy flying through the night like the monkey creatures in The Wizard of Oz, trying to find an open window. In one situation he had created in his mind, Monkeyboy was hiding in a pile of dirty clothes, and he jumped out and joined Asa in his bed.

Jerry answered the door before Asa got up the steps. He was in a pair of sweatpants and an old worn-out Stevie Nicks t-shirt. He looked tired.

"Come on in."

Asa nodded. Inside was the smell of cinnamon, medicine and cat-box. It was too warm.

"My mom's asleep," Jerry said. "I made a casserole and an apple pie." He giggled.

Asa sat down on the sofa, already feeling sleepy. Jerry sat down on piano stool in front of a small, dark upright with yellow keys.

"Hungry?" Jerry asked.

"Sure."

But Jerry did not move. Asa could hear the old woman snoring suddenly, just down the hall.

Jerry stood up and opened the lid on the piano stool. He took out a framed picture.

"I framed it," he said with pride.

Asa saw his pencil sketch inside a black frame meant for diplomas or birth certificates, the kind you get at the Dollar Store. The man's smile looked sinister now, as if he were mocking both of them. Asa stood and gave the picture back to Jerry.

"Looks pretty good."

He went over to the wall and looked at a picture of a little girl. It was in black and white and the girl had silvery blonde hair, thin and pale beside an ocean in a black one-piece, holding a shell. Jerry came over, after putting the picture back into the piano stool.

"That's mom when she was a little girl. She was a cutie-pie."

Asa turned around and saw Jerry walking down the hall. Jerry shut the door to his mom's room so they wouldn't hear her snoring. He walked back and smiled and grabbed Asa's hands.

"Come on into the kitchen."

After they ate, they went back to Jerry's room, passing the old woman's shut door. Jerry's bedroom was fancy, white walls and light blue carpeting.

"I'm so glad you came," Jerry said, shutting the door.

Asa stood by the large white bed. Jerry was unbuttoning his flannel shirt, pulling down his pants. His flesh was a blushed orange in the night-light. Eventually Jerry stood in his white underwear. The silence became everything in the world.

Asa walked toward him and kissed Jerry until they were on the bed together. Jerry began to claw at Asa's clothes, but Asa pushed his hands away, then helped Jerry strip from his under-wear. Naked, Jerry looked emaciated and misshapen, but his face beamed a new light, as if he now knew what it meant to be exactly what he was supposed to be.

Asa closed his eyes and began moving his lips down Jerry's arm. Suddenly they both heard Jerry's mother begin to moan. She got louder. Jerry put on his robe and walked to her room.

"Mom, you okay?" Jerry asked, tying the belt in a bow.

Asa followed and could only see the old woman's feet in the light from the half-open door. Bloated and slightly purple with crooked nails, slanted up on a plush white pillow like a display in a small boy's melancholy dream.

The next night, Asa went to his art class, but found out class had been canceled. The instructor was ill. Asa stood inside the old building, beside a hissing radiator. The rest of the school was closed. On a bulletin board above the radiator were drawings of different kinds of hands. He stared at them until they became blurry, then walked outside.

Asa hadn't been home since last night and had not slept either. He walked away from the building, down a sidewalk to an apartment building across the street. He looked for Eddie and Doug's mailbox, found their apartment number, and walked up and knocked on the door, wanting to run as soon as he heard something stirring.

Doug opened the door in raggedy t-shirt and sweatpants. "What?"

"Doug, it's me."

Doug glared at him. "Asa?"

"Yeah." Although he hardly knew Doug, Asa felt warm and nostalgic.

"Jesus. I thought you'd quit. You want to come in?" Doug asked.

"Yeah, sure."

The apartment was sparse, with cardboard boxes every-where. Only the TV and a mattress were unboxed, with a plate of half-eaten rice and beans on the floor beside an ashtray. The TV flashed extraterrestrial light across the boxes and floor. Asa stood above the mattress, and Doug flopped down, picking up his plate.

"Eddie's gone," Doug said. The fork scraped the plate.

"Where?"

Doug laughed snidely, eating. "Why do you care?"

"I don't know."

Doug continued to eat. In the movie, a pornography actress was doing a masturbation dance to help a man kill his wife. Asa watched it with Doug. He wanted desperately to tell Doug about Jerry and about what had happened. How he had drawn the naked man for Jerry, how he had kissed and was about to do other things to Jerry in his bedroom the moment before Jerry's mother had a big stroke. How all these things were combining to a dreamlike intensity that terrified him, how he knew he could never go home for some reason because of it, because of everything, because of now.

But all Asa could say, as Doug stood up, was, "Do you like Marilyn Monroe?"

Doug laughed. "I guess. I don't really think about her too much."

"There's something really creepy but sweet about her or something—I mean, outside of the fact that she killed herself, which is all people concentrate on. She looked dead way before that, but not unhappy about it," Asa said. "Like a wax figure or an angel. I've drawn her so many times now it's like I could draw her in my sleep."

Doug was in the kitchen, rinsing his plate.

"Eddie went to New York City. He thinks if he can make it there he can make it anywhere."

Doug stood in the doorway of the kitchen, his face strained and angry and hurt.

"Why didn't you go with him?"

Doug laughed solemnly. "Somebody else went with him."

"Oh. You miss him?"

Asa walked to him, and Doug walked back into the small kitchen. He looked Asa directly in the eyes.

"Yeah. I mean, yes. I miss him."

Doug stood above the sink, licking the edges of his goatee. It was a very small space, and Asa was very close to Doug. Doug was thin and had almost crossed eyes.

"There's this guy I know," Asa said, breathing into Doug's face. "I think he might be mentally ill. Or whatever I don't know.

Anyway, last night I went over to his house to have dinner with him, and his mom died."

Doug nodded his head. "That's sad."

"Yeah."

Doug walked out into the living room and sat down on the mattress. Asa followed him.

"And this guy," Asa said. "He went completely nuts in the emergency room. I went with him. And he started crying like a little kid, and a nurse had to come out and take him into a little room where she gave him a shot of something to calm him down."

"A shot? Really? I hate shots. Isn't that against the law?" Doug said. He didn't really seem interested, but at least he was being nice.

Asa sat down next to Doug on the mattress.

"I don't know. I left then," Asa said.

He realized there was nothing else to say about the whole thing.

They watched TV for a while. Asa felt very sleepy and fell back onto the mattress.

It was close to morning when Doug shook him awake, whispering, "I'm cold, are you?"

"Yeah."

Doug got a blanket out of one of the boxes and covered them both with it, and eventually they fell back to sleep.

BARRY

IN

THE

SCORCHED

GRASS

Barry eats cereal from an orange bowl, sitting Indian-style next to a swing-set. It is religious, the way he eats, dull-faced, his eyes almost closed. He does not wear a shirt with the green swim-trunks he slept in. His hair is black, cut short like a Cub Scout's, although completely uncombed.

Sitting on the patio, I imagine the cereal in Barry's bowl. Fluorescent fruit circles in discolored milk float up, then enter his mouth. He drinks it at the last, stands and stretches, picks his bowl up from the scorched grass, and flings it toward the house, running, and picking it up again. Although he tries to be friendly, Barry doesn't talk to me a lot. He never wanted a twenty-three-year-old stepbrother anyway. At sixteen, he only expects to get what's his and eventually grow up into someone who can stand this place long enough to get a job, get married, have a kid, and get a divorce so he can pretend to be sixteen again.

Before opening the sliding glass windows, Barry says, "Man it's gonna be hot." He doesn't look at me even though he seems to be addressing me.

I laugh nervously. "Oh yeah. Hot. Yeah. You're definitely right about that. Oh yeah. Hot, hot, hot."

Sometimes I can't shut up.

My mom is a nurse who goes from house to house taking care of people with extreme problems. Brittle diabetics, people with colostomy bags and feeding tubes that enter through their throats, emphysemiacs with oxygen tanks—all await her visits. She does not wear the traditional RN outfit, just clean pressed pastel shorts and a plaid blouse and her name-tag.

"Plans today?" she asks after I come in.

"Interview," I say.

"Where?" In the den beside the sofa, she's putting on her earrings, twisting in the backs.

"Guess."

She's angry for a second but laughs. "Hollywood, California."

"Close. Wendy's Old-fashioned Hamburgers Incorporated."

She doesn't say anything for a minute, fixing her watchband. Then she looks at me as if she is already exhausted.

"What do you want me to do, Dennis?"

I laugh, breaking down my sarcastic façade for her. "Nothing. I'm just going to my interview. I didn't ask you for anything per se."

I go into the den and flop down on the couch and turn on the TV. Mom sits down on the couch, facing me.

"Don't go. Just look in the paper on Sunday. There could be something in Cincinnati or Dayton. You need to get out of this town, I swear to God. There's nothing here."

I don't say anything. I can imagine the conversations Mom and her husband have in their plush bedroom down the hall, the worried excuses my mom gives, the heartfelt confessions from suntanned, balding Bob that he really can't stand me although he's tried so goddamned hard to be a second father to me.

"Don't go to Wendy's," she says. "You don't want a job like that."

"How about Kentucky Fried Chicken?" I say. "Isn't it Fortune 500?"

Mom laughs. "God, you get on my nerves, you really do." She stands up and grabs her medical bag. "I'm off to heal the sick." She stops and looks at me. "We'll look together on Sunday, okay?"

"Great. Whatever."

As she leaves, Barry comes into the den. He sits on the floor with the remote and flips through channels. After a few minutes,

Barry throws the remote into my lap and walks away without saying a word.

I push myself upright in the lounger and click the TV off.

Barry runs to the thermostat in the hall next to the stairs and turns the AC up, then goes over and stands in front of the patio doors, looking out at the backyard as a dog or cat might do. He has put on Nikes, no socks, unlaced, an old t-shirt. For a second I let my eyes linger on his shoulder-blades, spine, legs. Eventually Barry goes out the patio doors, walks down the backyard into another yard, and skips the fence.

After my shower, I do what I always do when no one else is around. Step into Barry's room and smell it: yeasty with dirty clothes, mixing in with the mildew of the AC, the residue of deodorant. Naked and half-wet, I slip into his bed, a twin with blue sheets, empty CD cases spread out. Lie down like a corpse, still and anxious, allowing my body to lose the rigidity after a while, sinking into the smell.

I crawl onto a cliff and fall off, letting myself for fifteen minutes pretend I'm him, or I'm his girlfriend, and I am what Barry actually dreams of. I am beautiful and desirable. The bed squeaks as I jack off, CD cases falling to the floor. I curl and uncurl my toes, whispering his name over and over like a spell to invite evil spirits in.

At dinner that night, Bob says, "Dennis, you had an interview, didn't you?" He smiles. He has a cracked, brown complexion and blue eyes, his hair, black with silver threads, combed back over the bald part. His tie is loose, his beige sleeves are rolled up.

"I decided not to go."

Barry is quiet, making a taco beside me. Bob looks over at Mom as she sits down.

"We're gonna look in the papers, Bob. On Sunday. Find something in Cincinnati, right?" She looks at me.

"Yes," I say.

Bob grabs a shell and stuffs it full of meat, cheese and lettuce.
He nods his head before he takes a bite, then bites it and squints,
as if he is thinking really hard. Chewing, he says, "Whatever you
guys decide."

Bob finishes the taco in three bites and makes another in
silent fury. I don't even wonder why he's so pissed anymore. At
college, I never thought I would graduate. There was an exciting
negligence to taking art history classes and writing checks for
cartons of cigarettes at the bookstore, buying pizzas on the Visa
Bob gave me.

Mom says, "Today was terrible." She smiles and nibbles. "I
had this one case. I swear to God. I can't even talk about it. I mean
I shouldn't. It would be unethical or whatever."

"What?" Bob asks.

"This poor old guy. I can't even say it."

Barry laughs, "What?"

Mom scoots up close to the table. "Well, it's a new case, and
I was going out to do an intake and all that. You know, just going
in to ask some quick questions. Anyway, I go in and this poor old
guy is living in squalor, just terrible. And he can't get out of bed.
Says his sister comes and checks on him and stuff, but then I pull
the covers off him, and he has the biggest decubitus I have ever
seen. I mean it was the size of this plate."

Barry looks mystified. "What's 'decubitus'?"

Bob belches into his hand. "Bedsore. Thanks a lot, Helen.
That really makes a meal like this go down swell."

Mom laughs and slaps her napkin at him. "You're a wuss. Bob,
I mean, get into the healthcare business. This sore was all over

his backside and you could almost see his hipbone. I had to call an ambulance to take him to the ER."

Mom looks at me for a second, and I smile at her. Her eyes glaze over as she seems to make the ironic connection between an old man with a terrible bedsore and her ambitionless fatty of a son. That fleeting connection has suddenly made her very angry I can tell, both at herself and at me, but the anger fades as she picks up her taco.

"Goodness," she says, before biting.

Barry gets up and opens the patio's sliding glass doors.

"Hey, bud, where you off to?" Bob asks.

"Down to Tony's. He's having a pool party." Barry is nonchalant, not looking at anyone.

"Good," Mom says. "A bunch of teenage boys drowning in the dark."

"It's lit outside, Helen," Barry says. "Helen" comes out with the same enthusiasm as "vacuum cleaner" or "toaster" would.

"Be careful, bud," says Bob.

I finish my taco. Bob ignores me. Mom puts dishes in the dishwasher, and I go upstairs to my room, which is still after two weeks the room of someone anticipating The Big Move. I close the door and slide out of my cut-off sweats and t-shirt, try to find a nice shirt and pants. After dressing, I go into the bathroom and splash on cologne, look at myself in the mirror above the sink. My face is moony, my hair cut short and neat, fingers plumply delicate, like a baker's. I try to see myself the way Bob would see me. It's real easy to do, have done it most of my life. Being overweight is a sign of an overall weakness and laziness. Something else too, but Bob can't quite put his finger on it: a terrible eagerness lingering in my eyes, a creepy hunger, a fury that might match his.

Downstairs Bob and Mom watch Entertainment Tonight, Mom on the couch, Bob on a lounger.

"Where you going, kiddo?" Mom asks.

"Out."

Bob laughs but says nothing.

"Don't stay out too late," Mom says after a few seconds. "You have your key?"

"Yeah," I say.

She smiles and turns her head away from me. I wonder if she ever imagines what I do at night. I walk down the hall thinking of it: all the faces, the woozy thrill of waiting to fall in love, finally settling for just getting really, really drunk and dancing like a lobotomized monkey.

Outside the heat is still thick. The sun is landing, purple light spreading over vinyl siding the color of Post-It notes. As I pull out in Mom's car, I see Barry and two friends walking up to a stoplight close to the subdivision.

"Hey," Barry says, motioning for me to unlock the door.

Barry and his friends, one blond, the other redheaded, get in. Barry sits in front.

"Can you take us over to the mall? Tony's pool-filter thingy is fucked. We can't swim." Barry smiles.

At first, I can't really process having Barry and his two friends in the car with me.

"Hey," Barry says as we get closer to the mall. "Dennis, would you mind doing us a favor?"

"What favor?"

Barry leans over toward me. "You're twenty-one, right?"

"Yes."

"Would you like mind buying us a sixer?"

"A six pack of beer?"

Barry laughs. "No, 7-Up. Of course, beer."

They laugh, but then we all go quiet. Eventually I pull into a convenience store parking lot, turn the engine off.

"Where are you guys gonna drink the beer?" I say.

Barry shrugs his shoulders. "I guess over at Tony's."

"I thought you wanted to go to the mall."

Barry laughs. "That was just to get into the car, man."

I look back at the two boys, and they plead with their faces too.

"So?" Barry asks.

"I get you a sixer, and you guys go back to Tony's, drink it, and get caught, and they ask you where you got the booze, and you say?"

Tony speaks up, "My parents are in Hawaii."

Barry moves in closer to me. "Be cool," he whispers angrily, accessing his Bob-like tendencies. It might be the first time we've ever looked into each other's faces.

"Okay," I say. "Under one condition."

"What?" Barry asks, getting extremely pissed now.

"You let me come with you guys and drink a few."

At first the boys are shocked, as shocked as I am, by my ability to negotiate this kind of deal. I guess loneliness has become a form of strength, or more like a trick I'm playing on myself.

They agree reluctantly. I walk toward the convenience store doors, and in the reflection I can see the three of them talking, as if they are trying to figure out a way to ditch me.

I have to drive into the cul-de-sac with lights off, so Bob or Mom won't notice. In the basement, Tony pulls the curtains shut, then turns on the lights. It seems like a ceremony. The room is long, with a couch, lounger, and entertainment center. A ceiling fan whirs. The three sit down on the sofa, and Barry pulls the beers out, a twelve-pack. In front of his friends, he seems wiser, the leader. He gives beers to his buddies, then I step over and grab one. We drink in silence. They do not want me here. I know that of course. I can feel the heat of shame rising out from the foam of the beer, but then a stubbornness arrives in my blood because I am fucking here with them ha-fucking-ha.

I imagine all three of them naked, rolling and wrestling. I go over to the lounger and sit down, a little shaky. Tony gets up and puts on some music, Rancid. Barry laughs and guzzles beer.

"Thanks," he says, tipping his can at me.

"No big deal."

Again we all go silent. One boy sits on the lounger, the other on the floor, Barry on the couch. I stand up, sipping the beer. The stereo is very loud.

Barry guzzles his, and gets another, saying, "Good stuff."

The other boys laugh and agree. I sit down on the couch.

"Hey, Tony, get out the tapes," Barry says.

Tony, the blond, looks terrified. He gives Barry a dirty look.

Barry looks at me, "You like Die Hard?"

Barry stands up and goes over to the stereo and TV unit, pulls out a pack of cigarettes from behind the shelving unit. He lights one with a lighter from his pocket. Tony stands too.

I says, "I guess so."

Barry laughs, mocking me, "'I guess so.'"

"Can I have a cigarette?" I ask.

Barry looks at me, smiling, "Sure."

He lifts his arm up holding the pack. I pull one out, and he tries to light it with his lighter but it's out.

"Upstairs," Tony says. "Use the stove."

"Upstairs?"

"Yeah. Or there might be matches in a drawer or something. Bring them down."

"Sure."

The kitchen glitters when I flick the lights on. It's the same kitchen that Bob and Mom have. I turn on one of the electric stove eye, then light my cigarette on the red coil. Smoking, I go to the basement steps and stand there for a moment, unable to go back down. I can hear them laughing. Maybe they are talking about me, or maybe it's just paranoia, or maybe I want to escape, but I can't leave, because this is what I want, to reveal myself to them. I already know the end result, though. I think of it as a porn story from a really dirty magazine: downstairs all three of them naked and jerking each other off, hungry boy faces, the TV flashing against beautiful flesh. The truth interrupts that imagery of course.

Postponing going back down there, I walk around up here, going into a bedroom in the back. The bedroom is all dark polished surfaces, plush fabrics in the moonlight. I go to the bed and smooth out the comforter, then stare into the fabric's Arabesque pattern. The cigarettes falls from my mouth accidentally. In the dark, I try to get it back, but it rolls and makes a black hole in the fabric. I pick it up and take it into the bathroom and flush it. I run out of the room, but as I go toward the basement I can see the burned hole in my head, like a little black mouth. I walk back to the bedroom and turn on the light and there it is on the mauve comforter like a canker sore. I unmake the bed and start to sweat, turning the comforter over in order to hide the hole. I put the pillows back, then turn out the light.

Breathing hard, I walk toward the basement, and suddenly Barry is standing almost in front of me. He has been watching.

"What are you doing?"

"Bathroom," I say.

"There's one in the basement," he says.

He's pissed at me. I was just supposed to fucking buy the booze didn't I get that? Buy the booze and disappear. And now here I am invading his friend's house, tearing up the bed his parents sleep in and dream in.

"Listen, I'm going," I say.

Barry stands in front of me, trying to block me, and I have to push him a little to get away.

"What the fuck were you doing?" he whispers. "Is there something wrong with you?"

I push him against the wall with a sudden burst of strength. I am almost choking Barry, and Barry is looking at me, pushing me back, but then I get into his face and I kiss his mouth so deeply it seems like I am trying to kill him with what I'm doing. He pushes at me hard. He hits me. I can't believe I am doing this, but it also feels as if I should have done this before, the final act of a desperate attempt to be alive, or maybe the beginning of a whole new beautiful existence outside of time and space.

When I release him, Barry tries to grab for me, but I'm too damn quick.

"You motherfucking faggot!" he screams.

I'm running out the door, into the night, like the bandit of love.

Bob is in his pajama bottoms in the den with his putter. He often has insomnia, and to cure it he putts a ball into a drinking glass, TV on without sound. I'm almost out of the room when he says, "Dennis."

"Yeah."

Bob looks at me with what seems to be real curiosity. I wonder if I am bleeding. He manages to smile, as if he is forgiving me for everything, including shit I didn't do.

"I just want to say that when I get a little gruff, you know, about a job and all that, it's just I'm thinking of your own good."

He is holding the putter across his stomach sideways. He laughs and licks the bottom of his mustache.

"Don't worry about it," I say and start to walk away.

This makes him mad.

"Wait," he says.

"Yeah?"

"Let me finish. I want to help you in any way I can. Just ask."

Bob walks over to me and extends his hand. We shake. I look at his face, thinking how he will never know me. There is a certain satisfaction in understanding that no one here in this house, in this neighborhood, will ever know me, not even Mom. I mean, for real. I see Barry's shocked face, like an animal seeing itself in a mirror for the first time, that dumb horror of recognition. The kiss I gave him still vibrates inside my mouth, and I wonder what Barry said to Tony and his other friend. Maybe he will be storming in the front door any second.

I will pack everything I own. Bob can buy Mom a new car.

Automatically Bob returns to his putting. I walk backward for a second. Bob keeps his head down, and the putter makes a slight click on the ball. The ball enters the drinking glass, and Bob congratulates himself, keeping his voice low so that I won't hear.

LILY
OF
THE
VALLEY

It isn't "love" in the dictionary sense of the word, or any sense of the word. It is just this guy, I mean this middle-aged probably whacked-out guy, standing at the cash register at the Goodwill Thrift-store, as I purchase a pair of used but still wearable work pants. I have never seen him before. At the register, I notice his name-tag: **WARREN**. I notice his dead, sad-sack smile. That's a good name for him, I'm thinking, and he is the assistant manager, according to the tag. I'm not saying a word. He has this almost vampire face as he checks out the pants, which are blue and slightly ragged.

Warren looks up at me and says, "One twenty-five, sweet-heart."

"Did you just start here?" I ask, not looking at him.

"Last week. Fresh meat," he says, smiling.

I smile. This is the moment of connection. I feel a little scared of him. He must sense this because he folds the pants as carefully as a suburban housewife on speed, to show me something about himself, how careful, how in control he is, but he isn't. He has the shakes, just enough to make him sexy. I think how pathetic he is, but that's only a defense mechanism: I wonder what he looks like naked, and that is disturbing but sweet, to think of him that way. He is tall and skinny and has outer-space alien eyes, has baldness starting on top, has thick strange sweet lips, almost purple, a nicked chin from sloppy shaving.

He puts the pants into a paper bag and I give him my money and it's over. Outside the air is so muggy my throat closes up, the sun throbbing through haze, glinting off car hoods and white litter. I light up a cigarette, then destroy it, look inside at him again as he takes a pen from behind his ear and marks something up. I'm thinking it's the heat, but then Warren sees me staring at him and suddenly he knows me, he knows my soul, the new guy who manages the Goodwill in Anderson, Indiana, knows my soul.

I take off, but soon return as if by an electromagnetic ray, this time buying a set of jelly glasses.

"Just a shopaholic." Warren's voice is smooth but stylishly gruff.

"I can't stop myself," I say.

"I don't blame you, hon."

He wets his lips, shutting his eyes for a moment of symbolism. I just stand there like an idiot experiencing the genius of a great actor without having any way to appreciate it. Yes: he smells good too. Unknown cologne, cigarettes, coffee breath. I lean in to him, closer. Two fat ladies at the checkout next to us, run by a tiny black woman, are buying baggy housedresses and record albums, giving us curious and disapproving stares.

"You've got to be kidding," Warren says as I pull back.

"What?"

"You're all of sixteen," he says.

"Twenty."

"Shhhhhh," he says. Then he laughs silently. He puts on his glasses to look at my fingernails.

"You keep them clean."

"Yeah."

Someone buys a naked baby doll. Another person buys seven old bowling trophies. I stand next to a basket of coat hangers, then look up at Warren as he turns around.

"This is the life."

"Yup," I say.

Warren stares at me for the longest time. My aunt will say something about my wanting to replace my father. I'll tell her she doesn't know what she's talking about.

"What do you like to eat, my friend?" he whispers.

"Anything," I say.

"I guess I'll need your name." He has a slapdash, movie-star elegance, squeezing out from the orange checkout, toward me.

"Jay," I say.

He stands beside me, inspecting my scalp. I pull back and see Warren seeing me. I can envision myself through his expression, how he thinks I am a little pathetic, too, too tall and gangly to be quote-unquote "attractive," with my dumb-ass Greenday t-shirt, my Birkenstocks and faded shorts, my slightly oily hair and, yes, offbeat, doughy complexion: a bookworm, a burgeoning pervert, and maybe he likes that.

"Jay," he pronounces.

"Yeah?"

"I think this could be one of those turning points."

I have no idea what he means, but I smile at him because it sounds hopeful and ominous. He pulls a skinny balloon out of his pants pocket and blows it up into a pink hotdog, and with a few twists and turns it's a dachshund, no shit, sitting there on the countertop.

I have to laugh. Warren pops the dog with a safety pin from his shirt pocket.

"I can create and I can destroy," he says in his best Charlton Heston.

I figure he must have balloons in his pocket just so he can say that. People standing in the tiny black woman's line are looking at Warren, but then looking away.

"Me, too," is my response.

So I found Warren on the day I bought work pants, on the day I was going to go in to work a little early to make some extra money but instead we went to his apartment at three-thirty and did it, did it till five-thirty. Then I had to call Loretta, the lady who owns Goldenhouse, the Chinese restaurant where I work. I told her I had the flu.

"The flu," however, turned out to be his apartment, the half-lit nausea of his little studio. Dirty clothes were everywhere and there were no pictures on the walls, and I was staring at a plate on his table covered in dried gravy as I told Loretta how sick I was.

"You better be sick," she said. Her accent was almost gone and came out only when she was totally pissed, like when the ex-con who did dishes busted plates or when her ex-husband came into the place wanting to borrow from the register. Then pure Chinese fury blasted out of her mouth, and she'd go all dragon on your ass, this four-foot lady with a black curly perm standing in a gold lame' top and polyester pants, wearing dangly earrings and lipstick the color of raw meat.

"Oh, God, Loretta, I feel like shit," I said. "I really do."

I hung up, and Warren was in bed still, smoking.

"I don't normally do this," he said.

"Yeah, I know," I said.

Naked, Warren appeared absurd, with his dark flesh sagging a little at the armpits, his chin hitting his chest as he continued to smoke in that awkward position in bed. Two cats came out of the bathroom and found a place next to him. Warren petted the fluffier one. The light from the blinds made zebra patterns across the blanket. I felt elegant and satiated.

Warren looked up and said, "Do you only tend to drift toward older men?"

"Wait a goddamned minute. Are you older?"

Warren found that amazingly funny. We started to fuck again. I looked at his face as he maneuvered into me. He was the ghost of the Shah of Iran suddenly, regal and debonair and a little terrified of himself, of his power. I was kissing the air around him, smelling him again, the creepy odor of his apartment, the gloomy light in here making it all seem like we were sinking into the ground, into a makeshift cemetery under the Iranian embassy where the corpses did this dance called fucking and everybody, even the people with their heads chopped off, was getting it on.

After, Warren sits up in bed like Nosferatu and tells me to get out.

"I need you to go."

"Why?"

"Issues of space."

He is not joking. He gets out of bed and goes into the bathroom and I hear the shower hiss on. I stand and try to get into the bathroom but he has locked it and then I hear him say through the door, "Do you need a place to stay?"

"Yes," I say, a lie.

"You can stay here as long as you go away when I tell you to."

"Fuck you!"

But I'm laughing.

Rita says, "Why do you want to move in with a total stranger?"

She is an amazing lady, I want to say first off, flabby and tired but still oddly and masculinely glamorous in her postal uniform with a cigarette in her mouth on the patio of her condo, like a character from a short story, her bangs hanging down over her shiny forehead, sunglasses shielding her eyes. She has knee-socks, a big mug of coffee, huge, comfortable boots, a wallet on a silver chain.

"Tell me," she says. "Go ahead. Explain this to me."

"Because."

If there is one thing Rita hates, it's when I'm trying to be cute. She backs up and gets ready to go back in, but I stop her by whining. She puts her cigarette out in her coffee mug and puts the mug on the rickety patio table where I sit in a robe and underwear.

"He's so creepy," I say.

"That's why you want to live with him?"

"Yeah. That's about it in a nutshell."

"Plus, he's an old man."

"Yeah, that, too."

Rita laughs at me, the aunt who took me in after my dad kicked me out. My mom, Rita's sister, died when I was ten, of pneumonia, a nurse who never went to the doctor, and then last year I was suddenly proud of being gay, one year out of high school and with this guy named Brad I met in Florida. Not a good match, but he was beautiful and he was willing. I came home and my dad blew up at me, out on the lawn, a fucking TV movie. Brad disappeared in the midst of the turmoil, and I came here to Rita's because she always knew what I was and I always knew what she was and it was nice like that, no place to hide, no need to. It still is. When she brings a friend over, usually a skinny blond lady with hazel or deep-blue eyes, I excuse myself, and then I imagine Rita whispering, "He's my nephew, the best kid in the world."

"You know what I think you ought to do?" Rita asks, retying her left boot.

"What?"

"Quit that shitty job. Quit hanging around downtown like some idiot. Quit burying yourself here and go to school. I'll loan you the money. You know that."

Rita does not look at me as she talks and I love her because she's not being a bitch about the whole thing, just concerned.

"How much can you loan me? A million?"

Rita laughs.

"It's weird," she says suddenly. Changing the subject is her specialty. She stands next to a beige gutter, looking out at her miniscule backyard. "It's weird to think that like three hundred or so people actually depend on me for their mail, you know? Me. Me with my prescription for Prozac and my fully loaded semiautomatic."

She smiles, not allowing herself to laugh at herself, and says, "I don't want you going to live with some strange man who manages a thrift-store and who is twice your age and who looks like Count Chocula, but hey, you're all grown up now, aren't you?"

I don't know if she's mad or giving me her blessing or what, but Rita disappears through the tall patio-window curtains, into the condo's kitchen, and I can hear her getting all her gear together, and then she's off to do her duty. I go upstairs and get ready to depart. I don't have much stuff, just uniforms for work, books, clothes. Downstairs I look at myself in the bathroom mirror before leaving and I see the wormy face of a lazy criminal, or the uncle you are afraid of; but also I have youth on my side, and this gives me a menacing glint in my eyes, pouty lips, smooth, shiny skin, a full head of hair.

I want Warren to see me as perfect, the perfect specimen. But then I think that I do need to go on with my life. I remember my dad, who was always miserable doing what he did, a car salesman who turned on the charm on the phone, even when he was about to give my mom the what-for: his skull of a face brightening up as he picked up the receiver, going into an automatic conversation with another car salesman about how much he'd sold, how much he was willing to do, and then hanging up and being totally quiet for a while, looking around at his house and knowing this was it: his life. You have to insert me somewhere in there, a scrawny little fuck complaining about a bike or a tree house, and then all grown up and coming up to him, and saying in his proudest voice, "I'm gay, Dad, and this is Brad."

I hated my dad anyway, so telling him was actually a release of all the manners I thought I was supposed to have. My telling him, though, did something to him, made him fall apart out of his car-salesman self, made him turn rigid as that one old fucking preacher on TBN. I have to admit I didn't think he had it in him to be righteous, self- or otherwise. I thought he would just ignore it and eventually have us over for dinner, Brad and me bringing over angel-food cake for dessert, with strawberries and fat-free whipped topping.

After all, Dad's has not been a sinless life. But faggotry does something to people. It makes them nervous about what they have, I guess, and there in the front yard with a cantaloupe-colored sky and the humidity at 85 percent and Brad staying in the car until I talked to Dad, and me swinging up to Dad as he came off the porch, almost first thing saying that about my being gay and being with Brad.

"You sick little fuck," Dad whispered. Or maybe he yelled.

He was flabby, his sleeves rolled up, his tie loose, and I was shocked. I thought my saying that up front would make him break out of his dreary life, not in this hateful way but in the melodramatic, self-pitying way of parents with gay children. He would learn to love me and to love Brad my partner (that's what he would end up calling Brad, in his pitiful, self-help voice), and then there he would be on Oprah talking about loving your kid no matter what and now he thinks of all of this as a great big beautiful blessing.

I stood there that day and I did not say anything to my dad and he said, his back turned to me as he walked up the porch steps, "You are not living here, buddy. Get your shit and get out of here. I won't have this."

Dad marched back inside the house. Brad was still in the car, embarrassed, staring away from me. Brad did not want this kind of shit in his life. He was too handsome, too clean for me anyway. I remembered meeting him on a beach, first noticing the back of his neck, the way the hair was trimmed so perfectly at the nape, wanting to taste the edge of his hair, and then I did it, and he had an All-American laugh, a family with three sisters, a dog who died of diabetes. As I walked back to the car, Brad disintegrated right before my eyes, beamed back to the mother-ship. The car was empty except for the sound of some nasal-voiced alternative rock singer singing a song about peaches.

When I arrive at Warren's, Warren is not there. An old lady is cleaning his apartment with the door open.

"Where's Warren?"

"He's out of here," she says, standing up straight, very pissed. "Got him evicted finally. That son of a bitch."

"Evicted?"

"Yessir. He does not like to pay his rent. So I had the sheriff come in this morning, and he kicked him out."

"Huh?"

"Yessir."

The old lady has a pasty look, in shorts and a Garth Brooks t-shirt, her hair bobby-pinned into an ornate cap of tiny curls. She is cleaning the sink and stove with gray water.

"You can find him at the track," she says.

"Track?"

"That horse track they just built down by the interstate. He goes there and blows his money. He's proud of it. He likes to tell me how much goddamned money he blows and then he asks me for an extension on his rent. Well, them goddamn days are over."

She laughs, going back to sticking her head into the oven. From inside the oven, I can hear her voice, "That son of a bitch."

Outside the horse track in Anderson, Indiana is a huge parking lot and a sign that says **YOU'LL HAVE A GOOD TIME YOU CAN BET ON IT**. The track is surrounded by newness: Applebee's and TGIF and a shopping mall and new bowling alley and cineplex – a whole new town, really, motels and apartments and housing divisions all looking like a computer-generated backdrop in an expensive blockbuster about to be blown up by European terrorists in Armani suits. I park for six bucks not knowing what I'm doing, just following the old lady's instructions. As I walk up to the main entrance I can hear bells and an echoed P.A. system. Inside, a race has just begun, satin-saddled horses throwing black dirt behind them on an oblong path. All around me are old people with nothing better to do than drink beer and smoke and throw away money, husbands and wives and lonely widowers and widows.

Suddenly I see Warren walking beside me with a cigarette in his mouth. He does not appear at all nervous. Everything is under control. At first, he tries not to recognize me. Then he does and he wants to avoid me. He approaches me finally.

"You into horses, too?"

"Not really."

Warren smiles. "I used to go to Kentucky all the time. Now I can go here. Thank God for convenience. This isn't a great track by any stretch of the imagination, but it does the job. I just bet two hundred on Lily of the Valley. The sweet little names they have here."

The sun is glaring off Warren's black glasses, and we stop beside a trash can. Sweat bees swarm round the can.

I say, "Didn't you just get evicted?"

"Yes, I believe I did."

He smiles again. He seems to be in complete control, killing a sweat bee with the palm of his hand, leading me to the top deck, where he watches the next race. Lily of the Valley finishes last.

"That was nothing," he says.

"Yeah. So where are you going to live?"

"You got any ideas?"

"Not really."

Warren wipes sweat off his forehead with a bandana from his pocket. "I've never been to Las Vegas. You'd think I would want to go to Vegas, but that just seems like a lot of hoo for nothing."

He stands up and stretches. I look at his face and I see something diabolical and innocent, a blend of teenaged boy and fifty-year-old mortician. He sits back in his seat.

"I go to sleep here sometimes. The sounds of the commotion put me to sleep, you know, like the way they say vacuum cleaners do for babies. I just sleep here and I wake up and I go bet. I only work at Goodwill twenty hours a week, so basically I'm here."

The Great Mystery, I think, then I get up, pissed at him, disappointed, thinking I have made my decision finally, that he is even more of a loser than I'd thought and I just don't have room for this kind of bull-shit in my little life.

As I turn my back to him, he says, "I'll pick you up tonight."

I turn around, but even before turning around, I feel myself give in automatically.

"What time?" he says, grinning.

"I get off at eleven."

"Eleven?"

"Yes."

"That's good."

"Pick me up at Goldenhouse, you know where that is?"

"Chinese downtown?"

"Yeah."

"Good."

Another race begins. Warren gets himself situated, lighting a smoke, smoothing back his dark, thinning hair.

———

It's a slow night at Goldenhouse, so I spend most of it sitting in a booth in back with a black Magic Marker, marking out the name and address of a Muncie Chinese restaurant on decorative paper placemats so that we can use them here on our tables. Loretta got them for free at some restaurant supply store. I've done four stacks before a single customer comes in. After that one customer, I sit down again. Loretta is doing paperwork at the cash register, in a lavender jogging outfit with silver lame' trim and big silver hoop earrings and mint green eye shadow.

"You got nothing to do?" she asks.

"I'm in love, Loretta," I yell back at her, taunting her, bored with blacking out.

Loretta laughs, shaking her head, not saying anything else.

"We'll end up closing early," she says finally.

"His name is Warren." I really do love torturing her sometimes to see how far I can go before she transforms into Mother Dragon. She does not approve of my gay lifestyle.

"Warren Beatty," I say. "He is the most charming man." (I'm using a Southern-belle accent now.)

Loretta says, "You burn in hell." She laughs a little.

"I thought this was hell."

"Close but no cigar."

Finally, I stop marking off the placemats and go outside to sweep. Downtown is completely dead, cocooned in the muggy promise of a storm. There's a huge movie theater from the forties, the State, next to us, the marquee orange and yellow neon, unlit and wordless but still glorious. All the other businesses on the block have also closed down. Everyone has gone out to the suburbs, to where the racetrack is, but Loretta has stayed here stubbornly. Now all's left is Goldenhouse, the Goodwill, the Section 8 office, a business-machine supply store. It does not fill me with sadness at all, being here with a broom confronted with all that vacancy, because I kind of get off on this solitary, glamorous feeling, the only sensitive person left on Earth.

Loretta comes out. She is smoking a long, long cigarette, looking dreamy-eyed.

"It's nice out here," she says.

I lean on the broom. There are no cars, no lights except for the greenish glow of the fluorescent **GOLDENHOUSE** sign. Loretta gives me one of her cigarettes, as is her custom, and we smoke and talk, she about her shitty ex-husband calling and telling her he owns half the restaurant, something he does every other week when he bounces a bunch of checks, and me about how maybe next year I'll go to college somewhere or buy a new car or buy something new. As we smoke, I feel like talking about Warren again, but I keep my mouth shut, and then finally Loretta says, "So, you really in love?"

She's sitting on an old wood bench with **FUCK YOU** scraped into it.

"Yes. This guy. He just started working at the Goodwill."

"He nice?"

She lights another smoke.

"Very."

"I read this article about how being gay is in your genes."

"Yeah."

"It still makes me sick," she says.

I laugh, and she lights my cigarette for me, and we sit in silence, watching the street, looking inside at the empty restaurant Loretta owns. It looks sad but comforting, like the way a mental patient might feel about the psych unit, all the tables and maroon booths in a row with the cloth napkins Loretta folds every morning into little tents, the silverware glinting in piles beside the menu board. On one wall is a beautiful painted peacock the size of a Christmas tree, its feathers spread out with little blinking lights embedded in them, a beautiful creation.

"I make you sick," I say.

"No," says Loretta. "Forget it. You're a nice boy." She touches my knee then, and I can tell she's trying hard to be my friend so I let her. It starts to rain slowly.

"Let's let it rain on us," she says, with the cigarette in her mouth, her eyes closed.

"Just a little," she whispers.

Warren picks me up in the alley behind the restaurant, after work. His car is a black Monte Carlo, the vinyl roof peeling off in black pieces. He opens the door from the inside, big-band music spilling out.

"This is weird," I say.

"You smell like sauerkraut," he says.

We are on the road to nowhere. I get nervous, looking at him. I wanted to explain how I felt to Loretta, as if by explaining it to someone easily disgusted it might make me see it anew, but now I'm glad it is a secret. This is what my whole life is and will be, a secret from everyone, even though no one really cares to hear the secret anyway.

Warren is tapping his fingers on the steering wheel. I like the smell of Old Spice (I figured out his cologne) and cigarettes and onion breath, I want to tell him. I remember his fucking me. I get all cozy inside, the way his cats must feel around him, and then I ask, "What about your cats? Did they get evicted, too?"

"She kept them," Warren says.

He parks behind the Goodwill and uses his key to get into the storage warehouse. We are assaulted by the musty smell of discarded crap: old beds and clothes and books and records and toys. He flicks a switch, and the whole place, about the size of a movie theater, flickers to life with fluorescence. There is a huge bed at the center, made with a crushed-red-velvet spread and several dirty-looking stuffed animals and elegant pillows on top. The headboard is garish French Provincial; beside the bed is a nightstand with a bottle of champagne in a cracked ice bucket.

"Our honeymoon suite," Warren says, his voice echoing.

I stare at the bed: it is the center of a huge dusty flower, all the stuff people don't want any more being the petals. I'm almost shocked. This must be Warren's way of loving me.

Warren turns the lights out after lighting one solitary candle. We walk together to the bed and he pours champagne into jelly glasses. It tastes vinegary and poisonous, but I partake. He gives me the candle.

"Watch me," he says, undressing.

I hold the candle up and watch him. His clothes seem to disappear, pulled into the shadows by little ghost hands. He is an old, sagging angel, or maybe Satan before the face-lift, who the fuck knows? But I do know one thing: I love him in a way I haven't loved anyone before, maybe since. We scoot all the stuffed animals off the red bed and then I strip, and in the dark warehouse we do whatever comes naturally.

Tomorrow I will awaken sticky and disoriented, will leave very quietly as Warren snores, stretched out like dinosaur bones in a museum. I will enter Aunt Rita's condo and take a shower, will have breakfast with Rita and Lucy, her new girlfriend with a white-blond perm and the crisp suntan of an aging movie-star about to do dinner theater, will eat sausage links and wedges of orange and drink coffee with heavy cream, will listen to Rita talk about taking in a boarder and Lucy talk about her own two grown sons, and I will feel bright and brand-new, knowing this is going to be my life for a little while, this person here is who I will be.

WITH

GARY

ON

A

WEDNESDAY

NIGHT

IN

LATE

AUGUST

Gary's apartment, as I remember it: an art-deco mirror above a white vinyl sofa, scarred from his light-a-cigarette-with-the-soaps-on-and-nod-off habit, a glass-topped coffee-table with cocaine scales and pictures in a shoe-box of his drag-days, two or three Polaroids of the pet monkey he dressed up when he was a kid in Kokomo. A yellow satin ball-gown on an organ-grinder sweetie. Leona was her name.

The screen-door is busted from his slamming it when he's pissed, which is a lot of the time. And outside are maple trees, kids on bikes in the dark jumping speed-bumps, sidewalks with old toys turning creepy in the glow of headlights. A rundown apartment complex in Speedway, Indiana.

The tiny kitchen has silver aluminum ice-trays everywhere, emptied for Gary's rum and Cokes, the dinette-table covered in rum bottles and new fresh bags of pork-rinds, his "sustenance," he says. Fashion magazines, half-filled glasses with the Jetsons on them, a huge TV, ash-trays always cleaned because he despises the smell of crushed cigarettes. A silver floor-lamp next to a little end table with Oral Roberts literature on it, mailed to him by his alcoholic aunt.

Kim and I are sitting on the floor here, Gary making a drink, hot as hell because running the air makes him sick, he says. Nothing blowing in through the windows except screaming kid noises and traffic sounds from the interstate and a moldy summer smell. Gary is in the kitchen. I can half-see him, in shiny maroon bicycle pants, black long hair all over the place like a fright-wig, flabby back, the sound of him pounding silver aluminum ice-trays on the counter.

Kim, my friend and his, calls, "You are going to break something Gary."

And Gary, a little serious, "Shut the fuck up Simone." He always called Kim "Simone" for some reason.

He comes out with his drink, sashaying, woozy. Pale and doped-up, Gary has a hairy chest, stubble on his big chin, a pure gas-station-attendant face, except for the beautifully-applied mascara and lip gloss. His bloodshot eyes throb, even though he keeps saying he is not sleepy goddammit. He hasn't slept for like 48 hours though. Too afraid, Kim whispered. He plops down beside me, smelling of Obsession and drug-sweat and pork-rinds.

"You do coke?" he asks me.

"No. Not really."

Gary laughs, a hoarse, wall-shaking laugh.

"Gary honey. Calm down," Kim says. "You need to go to sleep honey."

Kim is tiny, in a shorts and t-shirt, short brown hair, holding her drink, and Gary, gigantic, still laughing, reaches over to her and goes: "I love you Simone."

Gary was a guy Kim knew. She hung out with a guy who worked at TGI-Friday's, and this guy knew Gary, a special hairdresser for rich elderly ladies, but he broke the rules for Kim. Kim truly loved Gary, always talking about him, worrying about him, fighting with him. In a few months she would move in with him to help him.

This is the first night I met him, and Gary is going to cut our hair for us for free.

That night I was afraid but enamored. I'm gay too, buy Gary's gayness was luxurious, opulent and never-ending. I have to admit I was a little jealous too: me some shut-mouthed, uptight fuck in my lackluster clothes and dingy hair, having just got off work at Ponderosa Steakhouse. Plus Gary had AIDS, his t-cell count really really low, but I don't think I was totally afraid of him because of that. I was afraid of his style and mouthy, supernatural presence. Pulled toward him too.

So he cuts Kim's hair first, in the tiny dining room, with scissors from the kitchen. I sit on the splotchy cream-colored shag, watching.

Kim laughs, because Gary is swaying as he approaches her.

"You're gonna stab my eyes out," she says.

He snaps the scissors, laughs, turns toward me. "I get two-hundred bucks a pop for this, Keith honey. And she's fucking getting it for free and giving me lip."

I laugh too loudly, too much, covering up insecurity. After shaking his long, elegant fingers through Kim's hair, Gary starts the cut.

"That tickles," Kim says.

But the guy is totally fucking serious. He gets this face of a master, this Beethoven Hairstylist Face.

Gary says, "Shhhhhhh."

He cuts here and there, not using a comb or brush, just his fingers and scissors, and he steps back and looks and cuts a few more strands here and there. Then he runs back into the bathroom and comes out with electric sheers. Kim is laughing.

I just sit there, enraptured, as he does his magic sculpting and snipping, then the sheers buzz on and fill the room with a bee-hive hum. Gary shaves her neck with a magician's sweep, the back of her head, a little off the front. Turns the sheers off, saying, "Do not fuck with the master."

Kim feels the back of her head, still laughing, like she's been through a funhouse. Suddenly she's this New York performance artist only with a sense of humor.

I'm next. I sit down on the dinette chair. Gary is not talking, looking at his scissors. That face, that I'm-a-goddamned-genius face. I put my hands in my lap and close my eyes, and I can hear the bird-like snip of the scissors as he clips away my dark hair, flecks of it falling onto the tops of my hands, and I'm lost, looking intermittently at Gary, thinking he's like nobody I have ever known. Just doing this shit as if it is the most important thing in the world.

Kim's clapping as he turns on the sheers. The buzz going into my nerves like sugar, and I feel this drugged-up state coming from that buzzing, this luxury. I just let it simmer through me, let it glide into my head through my scalp.

"You are done, baby," Gary whispers soon after.

"What?" I say.

"You're done."

He coughs hoarsely, goes and lights up the longest cigarette I have ever seen. He flops down on the couch, looking at me.

Kim says, "You are so stylish Keith." She doesn't mean it, but I pretend I am anyway.

I look in the patio windows, seeing my reflection: I'm the guy from the Cure in a steakhouse uniform. Flushed cheeks, overweight, chapped lips, dull, after-work eyes, but then I see Gary get up and he comes toward me in the reflection. He fluffs up the style he just gave me. He kisses the top of my head.

Gary goes, "Not bad, motherfucker. Not bad."

He's talking to himself.

His pet-monkey still stays with me, of course. Leona.

Gary told us later, after he had snorted some coke with Kim, after he downed another drink, after Kim and I helped clean up the hair from the floor and then straightened up the rest of the place, Gary ordering us around as we collected clothes he had thrown all over the apartment: "That's dirty. That ain't. That's dirty but it goes to the dry-cleaner's." When we were in candle-light because the lights were bugging him now, looking at the drag-show and monkey Polaroids, Gary says, and I can still hear him even now:

"Monkey sister was a fucking bitch. Fucking bitch. Bit anybody. Mom made her that gown, that beautiful yellow gown, not just some everyday frock. This yellow sequined one to show her off in, and when Mom did that she ended up having to get a rabies shot. Leona would love running around the house all dressed up in that thing. You know, fucking prissy-assed princess, getting into cabinets, busting open a jar of marshmallow cream and just eating it like it was caviar. And when she died we had a funeral, you know, like in *Sunset Boulevard*, you guys ever see that? Before your time? Well anyway my uncle was a Methodist preacher, and he talked all about God's creatures great and small. I forget what else he said. It was just me and Daddy and Mom and two cousins, out behind our old house, sitting on kitchen chairs. Leona was in this box our neighbor made and we painted it pearly white. Pearly goddamn white! I remember thinking what was I gonna do with all Leona's clothes? All her everyday clothes. We buried the little bitch in that yellow dress though. The special dress. The one Leona, honey, would have worn to her prom."

I remember leaving the apartment with my new haircut, feeling like I was new-wave now, all funky and pretentious, despite the name-tag and the grease-stained polyester shirt. But also, more than anything else, feeling stunned and stupid.

Finishing his Leona story, Gary had finally crashed on his couch, with a lit cigarette of course. Kim had to take the cigarette from his hand, and then Gary curls up into a ball. Kim grabs a blanket from somewhere, and I am in the doorway, the door open. It's humid and very quiet this late. I get it suddenly: the main reason for our visit was to let him fall to sleep, to be here so he could talk himself to sleep. He needed an audience to do that I guess. It was so simple, too fucking simple probably, but still, even now, that dumb realization hurts, to think that Gary needed us there to go to sleep. That was all we could do.

Kim walks past, wordless, like leaving church. I look in there at Gary in his world, his white and silver, art-deco, cigarette-singed, coked-up-and-asleep universe. Gary snoring extravagantly. For a while this was all I could see.

FEAST

Wednesday, they could be seen walking beside the road, two young guys in dumpy clothes carrying heavy plastic grocery sacks. The sky was beige and snowy, the area flat with a strip-mall parking lot and dead trees. The stockier one was named Carson, the taller and thinner one Brad. Their apartment complex was just beyond the strip-mall, and inside the complex muddy paths snaked from building to building.

"All the trees are brown," Carson started singing. "And the sky is gray."

Brad said, laughing, "Please, please don't sing. Do not fucking sing."

Carson continued to sing his heart out, all the way to their one-bedroom apartment. Inside was what you might expect. Lumpy sofa. Posters of *Citizen Kane*, The Smiths, Antonio Sabato, Jr. smiling in a Calvin Klein underwear ad, an Escher print, black ducks transforming into white ones. They got the Escher print one afternoon at a head-shop while buying a beautiful blue bong that Carson eventually lost somewhere. A pickle jar filled with pennies and nickels. A bean bag chair losing its Styrofoam beans. It smelled bad, old smoke and the sour dark scent of dirty clothes turning mildewy. The bedroom had a mattress on the floor and stacks of old textbooks that someday they were going to return to the bookstore for cash, as neither of them went any more to the community college where they had met two years ago.

They put the food into the kitchenette, and then Brad sat down on the beanbag and lit a Salem Light.

"Get your ass in here," Carson said, faced with the task of putting up all the food. But he was only joking. He loved the abundance of food.

"You're the one who fucking wanted Thanksgiving," Carson said.

"You did too," Brad said.

"I don't really give a shit," he lied.

Carson looked lovingly at the huge frozen turkey, then out at Brad who was blowing smoke-rings. Outside the window, three kids passed in winter-coats, screaming and laughing. It went completely dark as Carson put the turkey into a sink of water to thaw. Brad started watching a fuzzy version of Wheel of Fortune. It was raining freezing rain.

"Give me a cigarette lazy-ass," Carson said, flopping down beside Brad on the beanbag.

They smoked, then both drifted into drowsy calm. Carson imagined what cooking all the food would be like because he had never done Thanksgiving before and Brad couldn't cook and God would he miss Brad, and Brad was thinking of his sister and how his sister last week when she asked him to come over for Thanksgiving told him not to bring Carson, and Carson was thinking of candied yams which they had purchased in big heavy cans and in the grocery store he had thought about what people must think of them, two dumb fucks buying a turkey and all the trimmings, but no one cared really. At the check-out, the cashier said without inflection, "Some feast."

Brad rolled over, looking at Carson. They pushed their faces together and kissed until Brad could almost taste whatever Carson was tasting, a mix of cigarette smoke and sour breath. Then they got naked. Brad licked around Carson's lips and chin, the silence inside the apartment almost like what might be inside a sealed envelope. This silence made their pleasure seem special, an eerie happiness because of it right then, Carson touching Brad's hair, Brad's tongue in his belly-button. All the food they just bought connected to the sex they were about to have, and then Carson went half-moon with his body so they could suck each other at the same time. They kept it up until they came at almost the same moment.

After, Carson fell asleep.

Brad went into the bedroom and got on the phone.

"We're not showing up tomorrow," Brad told Liz, his sister.

"You're welcome," Liz said.

"Not without Car," he said.

No response.

"Why?" Liz said.

"Why what?"

"Why do you stand by that son of a bitch?"

"Come on," he said.

"Whatever. Happy Thanksgiving," Liz said and hung up.

Lying on the mattress, Brad watched the ceiling for a while. Outside the window all he could see were bare tree-limbs cracking against black sky, frozen rain glowing like glass against the branches. They woke up around midnight. Smoked some pot and got naked again, kissing but not going anywhere with it. Finally, still naked, they watched Comedy Central while they still had cable, drank Car's favorite, Peppermint Schnapps from the bottle, until they fell asleep against each other.

Thursday Carson got up before dawn, after sleeping only three hours. He showered and stuck the thawed turkey into the oven. He read the directions on the Stove-top Stuffing box, then decided to take a smoke break. In the apartment, he felt so safe, and within this safety, Carson imagined what he looked like the day the cops came over. It was like very peaceful, being arrested. He looked into the peephole. He saw them, and thought, Should I run? He thought about talking his way through, but in the end he just opened the door and they came in and in a stilted voice the black-guy officer read him his rights and they didn't even handcuff him. They just escorted him up the cement stairwell to the cruiser.

It was $4500 in bad checks. Carson wrote them on two different accounts, one closed, the other one totally made up. The ease with which some tellers and cashiers accepted his checks had given him a sense of pride and self-reliance, as if he had an aura about him, as if he could just like go up to people and fuck with them and it would be, "Go right ahead. We love being fucked with by you, kind sir."

But on Monday he was going to court and then probably to jail.

"Brad," Car said, smoking, looking out the window. It was snowing now.

"Brad!"

Brad was dead to the world. Car got a whiff of the turkey cooking, and then it was like he got demonic amounts of energy and started making instant mashed potatoes and cooking stuffing and baking rolls and by nine-thirty in the morning it was ready and he made Brad get out of bed and eat.

"This fucking early?" Brad said, terrified at the sight of all that food sitting everywhere: bowls of corn and peas on the carpet, a turkey that looked as if it had been pulled apart and then put back together sitting in the corner on two paper plates, mashed potatoes, stuffing, yams, the whole nine yards just everywhere.

"Buffet-style," Car said.

At one point in the day-long meal, Car started feeding Brad kernels of corn one at a time like the way a Roman emperor would be fed grapes by his slave, and Brad said, "You are so full of shit Car," and Car said, "Yes sir."

Then Carson stopped doing the corn thing. All of a sudden, he looked like a rat in a cabinet when the cabinet door opens, all caught and dim-eyed and scared.

"Feast before famine," Car said.

Brad kept his mouth shut.

"Feast!" Car yelled, so horny it made the food go bad in his stomach.

A total ache opened up inside him like a crater. He crawled over to Brad and took Brad's pants off, like he was changing a baby's diaper. Car then put some mashed-potatoes on his finger and spread Brad's legs, and Brad gulped, "What the fuck is this, man? Nine and a Half Weeks?"

Which made them laugh, but they did not stop.

The mashed potatoes felt totally weird, warm and gushy going up, but at the center was Car's finger, and there were more potatoes, until Brad felt like he'd just shit his pants. The Car started eating the potatoes there, lying on his stomach, hungry as hell. The potatoes filled his mouth, and his tongue dug up into Brad. Car could not stop. Brad started moaning and jacking himself off, thoughtless with it, also aware how stupid it might appear to strangers. But then again, it was stupid only from the outside looking in. Inside, it was beautiful. It was all they could do. Like Car was eating him alive, Brad thought, and then he stopped thinking about any of it.

A
PLANET
CALLED
EUGENE

We are on our way to see *Alien*. It's July, a Friday night, 1979. I don't tell Eugene and his mom, but this will be my first R-rated movie, which adds a whole other level of luxury, on top of staying all night with him. Eugene and I are both fourteen. In the station wagon is the sleepy fume of his mom's cigarette smoke mixing in with the air conditioner's chill. A large woman who works nights at Delco-Remy, his mom has a rule: the radio has to be on an easy-listening station. Right now, we listen to Perry Como's rendition of "Yesterday."

"I can't wait to see this," Eugene says, turning around. I smile up at him, nodding my head in the backseat. Skinny and lanky, Eugene has a red, chapped mouth, black hair cut short with bangs just above the eyebrows. His eyes are dark and always darting, as if they have a different kind of energy than the rest of his face, an excitement he wants to keep secret. We don't ever talk much in front of his mom. Right away, he turns back around, getting into her purse without her seeing, stealing a pack of Winstons.

At the movies, Eugene's mom escorts us in, because of the R-rating. She buys the tickets, gives them to us, tells us not to get too scared, and then walks back out to drive herself to bingo. Eugene and I enter the theater alone. From the beginning, Alien doesn't really seem like a movie. It's more of an experience, a fever Eugene and I share like conjoined twins.

Grim, sleep-eyed astronauts wake up prematurely from hyper-sleep, sip their morning coffee as they drift through space, get a distress call, land on a gas-green planet with howling winds, investigate a huge cavern filled with neon jelly eggs. A uni-tentacled octopus sprouts from one egg onto an astronaut's face, and slithers down his throat to impregnate him.

All of this comes at us in dream form, a nightmare Bible story.

And all I know is I want to be with Eugene, witnessing this. I keep looking over at him as the movie unfolds, his open-mouthed joy at the serious metallic weirdness of it all. *Alien* is way more important to our lives than reality. It's a religion, the images on the screen laced with the ominous silence surrounding what we are going to do later that night. Right at that moment, I know how much I love Eugene. I know that what we will end up doing in his bedroom will only make the love grow deeper, into a black hole. I will come out the other end on a planet called Eugene, a planet that will have a smell like the smell coming from the movie theater's a-c vent, chilly blue mildew being the only atmosphere of this planet, the only substance your lungs can take in.

After *Alien*, we walk to the mall across the parking lot, smoking Eugene's mom's Winstons.

"That movie was fucking incredible," Eugene says.

I can't really talk about it, can't find the words to tell him what it means to me. We walk around the mall before going in, kicking at weeds sprouting out of concrete, lit by security lights. Rusty dumpsters, concrete bays for semi-trucks, the backs of brick buildings, all this makes me want to kiss him. By the way, I am pure white-trash too, with a Fundamentalist Baptist mom who works at Kentucky Fried Chicken and a dad who works for Indiana Gas Company reading meters. I'm sort of effeminate too, but that gets canceled out because I'm trash and nobody pays that much attention to me anyway.

Inside the mall, we go to the record store by JC Penney. We take ELO's *Greatest Hits* and *Tusk* by Fleetwood Mac, eight-tracks, from the shelf, go over to where the poster racks are, hide behind them, and put the tapes inside our jeans, pulling our shirts over the lumps. Eugene's eyes seem to go back deeper into his skull when he shoplifts, like he can see backwards, toward the security guards. We've perfected this system over the past year, and it always works.

We inspect the tapes in the middle of the mall, by a water fountain that doesn't have any water in it. Eugene lifts Tusk up, grinning. Even though we both ripped them off, he says, "You can have this one."

"Thanks," I say.

He gets an allowance of ten bucks a week, and his mom is buying him comic books all the time, so shoplifting isn't about getting what he wants, exactly. It's about doing something he can get away with. I idolize this lack of need, the suburban decadence of it.

As soon as we see Eugene's mom walking toward us, we hide the shit we stole. She doesn't seem to care. She never really notices anything, just wants to get stuff over with quick.

"You guys ready?" she says. Her eyes are totally bloodshot, the lids swollen. I wonder if she really went to bingo. I can smell booze on her, but now she's smiling in front of us, great big.

"You want pizza?" she says, a fake, almost strangled happiness in her voice, a divorcee getting over her divorce, a workaholic just trying to relax.

"You wanna smoke?" Eugene asks.

"Sure."

After we eat at Pizza Hut we go back to his house and watch TV, then end up going to his room so we can listen to the music we ripped off in the dark.

Eugene's mom is in her bedroom next door now, coughing, and Eugene's older brother, the one with sideburns who works at UPS, is in the kitchen, making something to eat. Electric Light Orchestra plays "Strange Magic." I am on the floor in my sleeping bag, Eugene up on his bed, one of those old-school waterbeds with a big flabby mattress. He got it for Christmas. Last year he painted his walls black, to simulate outer space. I stand up. Spaceship models he glued together dangle from the black ceiling on kite string.

He opens the window, turns on the fan. We light up, Eugene on his knees, leaning against the headboard, me next to him, standing on the floor. Outside his window are trees and tarmac roads and other houses glowing in street and porch lights. Anonymous ranch-styles with trim lawns and basketball hoops, not really rich or even upper-middle-class, but elegant and out of reach.

The moments right before we settle down to it, before I pretend to mumble in my sleep, are like Christmas Eve, two kids waiting on Santa Claus, other moments when you have nothing to live for but what is going to happen next.

Eugene says, "If she smells this, we're fucked."

The end of his cigarette glows red, mixing in with the green light shining from the stereo. In that light, he looks like somebody I don't know, and I don't, not in any real way. I wonder then why he likes me, a fat white-trash kid barely making it through school. But I get it too. Nobody else likes him.

"Keith?" he whispers.

I keep my eyes mostly shut, turning over to see him in the moonlight.

"You sleeping?" Eugene says.

I whisper, "Yes."

There he is, up there, floating on his stupid waterbed. I crawl up to the bed from my sleeping bag.

"Come here," Eugene whispers.

I move over to him. The next morning, we will be just like anybody else on earth. You need this to be in control of yourself the rest of the time, though, to know there is someone else, some other way to be, inside you, and it comes out like this.

Eugene whispers, "Keith, hey, get on your stomach. Come on."

I do. My face is pressed into the vinyl of the sloshy mattress. He is on top of me, and then slips it in. He kisses the back of my neck, maybe accidentally. He fucks like he wants to get it over with but also wants it to last forever, and I let that same feeling soak through me, that joy of being caught in a trap on purpose. I keep flashing on random images from Alien too. The way the octopus-thing jumps from the egg, the way the baby alien screams when it first pops out of the guy's chest, like it is lost and wants to go back in.

After he finishes, I jerk off while he gets up and goes into the bathroom to clean himself off. I come before he walks back into the room. He throws me a couple of Kleenexes.

The next day is a Saturday. Eugene has to get to his karate class and if they were to take me home he'd be late.

I tell him and his mom that my mom's on her way to pick me up anyway. Looking clean and angelic in his white pajama-like karate uniform, Eugene waves at me from inside the car, then looks away. His mom tells me, "You're always welcome here, kiddo." She slams the door. I smile, sitting on the steps next to my grocery sack of dirty clothes, watching the station wagon disappear.

Inside the house, Eugene's brother is playing his stereo, Led Zeppelin's "Dancing Days." There's a hypnosis to it. I just want to crawl back into Eugene's bedroom and hide there, wait for him to come home to me.

When Mom does arrive, it's in the Vega without the muffler.

You can hear her a mile off. She pulls up the driveway in her red polyester KFC uniform, my little sister beside her, wearing pink sunglasses she got at K-Mart.

I get in the car, smelling the fumes from the missing muffler. In the rearview mirror, I see my sister in the backseat, clapping her hands for no reason. Her sunglasses piss me off. They make her look stupidly innocent, like she's grasping for something glamorous she'll never have, grasping but not knowing she's grasping.

"You hungry?" Mom says, putting it in reverse.

"No," I say, not looking at her.

My little sister says, "I am."

I look up as Mom backs out, the engine ringing in my ears. That big brick house there in my vision, all I can really see, as we go down the hill backward, back out onto the road, back home.

JAMBOREE

When Carson got out of jail early that summer, the grocery store by their apartment complex was having a fair in its parking lot, almost like they were giving Car a homecoming.

Brad had gone to see Car in jail throughout his stint, but toward the end he got busy working two jobs to keep up with the rent. He was late picking Carson up, and Car was acting all pissed, looking destroyed yet happy, pale and yet very much alive, waiting on a bench outside the correctional facility in the same clothes he had worn in: jean jacket (even though it was hot), Nikes, cuffed work pants and his Scream 2 t-shirt.

He looked up as soon as Brad stopped the car and mouthed, "Where'd you get that?"

The car was from Brad's sister, Liz. When she'd let him borrow it, she hadn't known he was coming here. Liz thought, in fact, that he wasn't going to have anything else to do with Carson.

"Never mind," Brad said, opening the door.

Climbing into the passenger seat, Carson felt upset that there was actually a new car in Brad's life, like Brad had found fame and riches on the outside while he rotted and wasted away inside the Lebanon Ohio Correctional Facility. He could tell Brad some things about some of the guys in there and what it did to your brain—or he could tell him about the guy who had a secret stash of Doritos and Hershey bars and a joint or two and this volatile nowhere they shared for five days before the dude and some other guy got caught. And thank God it was with some other guy.

Carson gave him attitude from the get-go.

"Fucking waiting to go home, man. The whole afternoon. I mean I get out and then I have to fucking wait. That's so perfect."

It was like he was talking to himself, maybe something he'd learned in prison. Brad felt a ticking in his head like a time bomb and it maybe had something to do with horniness and nostalgia mixed. He wanted to kiss Carson but he also had worries about what seven months in prison could do to somebody.

"You hungry?" Brad asked him.

Car could not find words. He was not a hardened fucking criminal, so being outside meant something, you know? Waiting out there for his thoughtless boyfriend to come pick him up while he could still hear the PA system from the courtyard inside the prison, and see the people passing by, and it was like, Look I'm free you motherfuckers, but nobody noticed.

Um. Hell yes he was hungry.

Car remembered the Thanksgiving Day feast he had pre-pared the night before he had to go for sentencing. Turkey and dressing and corn and peas and pumpkin pie and mashed potatoes. And sometimes when he was with the Doritos guy Car imagined it was Brad, and it was that innocent debauched evening with freezing rain and nobody around to see. Surveil-lance just simply disappeared. And the Doritos guy, a pot-bellied Mexican fellow, turned into Brad—tall, skinny and beautiful.

"Hell yes I'm hungry," Car said, not making eye contact.

Brad drove down the country road, thinking about how all he could do was work when Car was gone, work two jobs, one at the laundry and one at the chili place next door to the laundry. In the work Brad found this special secrecy, like he was a war widow or something, his husband in war-torn Vietnam, maybe dead, and he couldn't tell anyone how he felt because he knew it was kind of a stupid story. This guy I love wrote some bad checks and now he's in jail and I still love him so much, in fact more because he's in prison.

Brad went to a drive-thru place on the way home and got Car what he wanted: "Two Big Macs, one large fry, a vanilla shake and a Coke. Super-size the fries, man."

Even Car's voice was different, a put-on machismo he'd had to adopt to keep from getting fucked with. They never talked about that kind of crap during Brad's visits. The couple of letters Car sent were short but sweet: "Today I mopped every inch of this place." Or: "This one guy stabbed this other guy with a piece of glass." Stuff like that.

They got the food from the window, and Brad pulled out. Car took a whiff of that familiar fried grease odor, could even smell the lettuce and the goddamn special sauce through the wax wrapping and paper sack. He wanted to cry. Sometimes pleasure gets distilled into tiny, excellent moments other people would just laugh at, like the ex-con ordering two Big Macs and then getting off just on the smell. Car decided to wait till they got home to eat it because he wanted to be civilized now that he was out.

"So you feel okay?" Brad asked.

"I guess," Car said, still smelling the food.

"You look good."

"Thanks."

Car saw the rides and booths of the fair in the supermarket parking lot as soon as they pulled into the complex. No one was waiting in line yet. It was almost dusk and the neon lights were on, the orange, blue and pink lights and the little tents and the chicken wire that surrounded the dunk tank. The people who ran it were still setting up stuff. It filled Car with a joy and an ache to see this. He smiled, with the bag of McDonald's on his lap. There was a big flapping sign tied up to two makeshift poles in front of the fair: **JUNE JAMBOREE**.

Brad looked over at Carson, as he drove past the fair into the parking lot. He resembled some beautiful child from a foreign country, an innocent awe in his gaze with his big sack of American food. He couldn't tell anybody how happy he was because he didn't speak the language. But he was so happy to be alive, it could make other people uncomfortable.

At the apartment complex, they parked and got out in silence. Inside the place was exactly the same. The same posters and rundown beanbag chair and thrift-store couch, except now everything had a nice order to it. Like in his absence Brad had gotten his shit together.

Carson sat down on the floor, Indian-style, unpacked his feast, embarrassed at being so happy.

"Didn't you want anything?" Car said, looking up.

Brad smiled down at him and got on the floor with him and they finally kissed. The connection between them was something Brad had jerked off to and thought about and talked to himself about. He would even call his sister Liz just to piss her off and whine about how much he missed Car and she would eventually hang up on him.

Brad just sometimes needed to say Car's name aloud. There weren't too many people who cared—not that Liz cared—but at least she knew who Car was. She would say, "I don't want to hear it, Brad." But Brad would say, "He was always wanting to do it, Liz and so was I. It was like we needed to do it, you know?" And she would get all irritated and Brad would laugh. And then click.

Brad pushed Carson back onto the floor. He felt an animal's bravery and stupidity. He took Car's clothes off and Car moved to let him, not even laughing.

And Brad took one of the Big Macs, undid the thing into parts, and started feeding each part of the thing to Carson one morsel at a time: the soggy special sauce-drenched bun, the lettuce leaf sliding into Carson's baby-bird mouth. Brad got naked too, then did the first hamburger patty, and he watched Car's mouth open as he inserted the hamburger slowly. Carson nibbled at it and he had the hugest hard-on and there was no laughing, just the silence of feeding your ex-con boyfriend a Big Mac in a silent movie way.

Then the bun between the patties, soaked with grease, then the other patty and cheese getting all over Brad's fingers, and the bottom bun and each fucking French fry.

Mouth stuffed, Car said, "I need something to drink."

"Wait," Brad said. His voice felt rough coming out, and he realized he was imitating some tough prisoner, some guy Car might have fucked in prison, and he liked the sensation of being Car's desperate equal, in the same situation, doing this.

Carson laid there, hard-on and everything, and Brad got his drink and pretended Carson was a hospital patient in a porn movie, helpless as a baby with a broken neck after a car accident. He let Carson suck on the milkshake straw and then Brad went down rough on him and he would look up and see Car sucking on the milkshake and taking breaks from drinking, Car would moan out his pleasure, some of the shake dribbling down his chin, and Brad could not stop, filling his mouth up with this fragile invalid's dick, this freak he missed so much. So much it had made his life seem lifeless, made his days seem endless and blank. And when Car came in Brad's mouth, Brad felt an erotic haze seep through what had been reality, all the months of working two jobs and waiting and all the blankness and fear melting into that taste and that texture, smooth and gummy and thick, and he swallowed it all, thinking of what they would do that night and the next night and the next.

Car wanted to go to the Jamboree.

So they did, after taking a shower and dressing in jean cutoffs and T-shirts and Nikes without socks. It was humid and the whole area was lit up from the rides, light scattering across ditches and trees and parked cars. They were quiet, walking

THIS IS TRUE LOVE

across the back of the complex. Brad almost felt the urge to hold hands but that was so fucking corny. He just watched Car's face as they made it to the front of the fair, child-like and dim. Car was not smart, never had been, but he knew what he wanted, and that always seemed better than intelligence to Brad.

"This is so goddamn cheesy," Car kept saying, but he was lying.

"Fucking people get killed on these cheap rides," Brad said.

But they rode the Tilt-A-Whirl, and the makeshift roller-coaster, The Happy Dragon. It was with a bunch of loud-mouthed kids, but Car fit in, screaming louder than everybody, and then they got some elephant ears and lemonade and brats, ate them like they were starved, and Brad didn't know where the fuck Car put it all, after eating all that McDonald's.

They walked around where the games were. Car of course paid ten bucks to win some dumb toy that he gave to a little girl, and right when they were going to go back to the rollercoaster was when Liz and her daughter Joy showed up, standing by the front gates to the place. Joy was a fat little three-year-old with red hair, and Liz was tall and pale, sucking on a big long cigarette, her hair tied back with a scarf.

Brad saw them first and wanted to steer clear, but Joy came running over. Liz followed right behind her.

Liz stared at him, "Where's my car?"

"At the apartment," Brad said, stunned.

"I was gonna let Joy ride a couple rides and then walk over and get it," she said. She was looking at Car, and Car was looking right back at her.

"Hey there Liz," he said.

She didn't say anything to him.

Brad walked over to Car. They were outdoors, but he felt foolish and nasty and alive in front of his sister.

Car felt as if he were in a post-correctional facility dream, in all the lurid colors of a jamboree and there that bitch was and then pow! Brad stepped up to him without a smile on his face and just planted one on Car's mouth. All their secrets seemed opened wide, wind-blown and dumbstruck like a fool getting off a rollercoaster.

Brad pulled away but Car felt it too, the situation unfurling, the moment in the heat, and he took Brad into his arms really hard and tongue-kissed him back after dipping him like old time Fred Astaire shit.

By this time, people at the fair were watching.

Brad looked at Liz. She was horror-struck, grabbing for Joy, hiding her eyes. After they split apart, laughing both of them, they noticed other people were looking and laughing and a few people looked like they wished they had guns.

But Car and Brad just laughed, out of breath, stunned by themselves.

"I just got out of jail!" Car yelled.

And then the two of them ran from the Jamboree back to the apartment.

FRUITCAKE'S
FIRST
OFFICIAL
MURDER
POEM

I just got done writing my first official murder poem. I show it to Mom and she says, "What in the world?"

I tell her, "Mom, this is my first official murder poem."

"Get out of town. That's not right." She laughs and looks over at the clock, giving the first official murder poem back to me. "Why aren't you at work?"

We're sitting in the kitchen. This is government-run apartments for the lower-incomes so there's beige linoleum always cold on your feet everywhere. She puts rugs down from the Dollar Store but still it's cold. I glance down at this floor littered with wadded-up murder poems that just did not cut the mustard. This one, this one right here in my hand, folded perfectly and shoved into a white oblong envelope with "To Doug" written in all capital letters on the front, this is the actual official murder poem I am going to give him.

"You are gonna get fired."

She closes her lips real tight. She knows everything. She is wearing a big wig that makes her look slightly clown-like. She's fat and in her teddy-bear nightgown. Her skin looks like the color of pineapple sherbet. Mom's got a disability, and she likes lording it over me that she don't have to work and I do.

"You are gonna get fired, buddy."

"No I won't." I laugh too loud, satisfied with my project here.

I know Doug will be kind of shocked, but that is the price a son of a bitch pays for leaving for the Army.

We have watched so much TV together, me and him, I was thinking we were a TV show. He is a good-looking son of a bitch. He carried himself quite well in his apron and chef's hat. He gives me all-knowing looks over the fires of the grill. Me a lowly busboy. Me a dishwasher without a name-tag. He runs the place, even though the managers think they do. He lives in Building C and me and Mom occupy Building D. It was meant to be, that is what I've been thinking ever since he gave me that first ride home and I asked him to come in and watch my WWF video on

TV at 2 am, and he did and we watched the Rock and Deathrod, and then he looks at me while I rewind the tape and he says, "All that wrestling is so fake."

Then he comes over and he drops me down on the linoleum floor and puts me in a headlock and I cannot breathe but, hello, this is true love.

Finally I break apart from his grasp and Mom comes into the room with her eyes half shut, this time in her see-through nightgown she bought at Fredericks of Hollywood just in case, but there is at this time no man in her life.

"Goddammit Larry. What is going on here?"

"A little wrestling match," I say.

"Well who is your friend?" She smiles like a mother-cat feeding all her new but invisible kittens.

Doug gets up from the floor. He is short and compact, like a toy made for small hands in a tiny world. He is muscular and calm and altogether all right.

"Douglas Moon," he says, and he goes over and talks to my mom with a gentleness that is refreshing in this area. He tells her he and his sister live in Building C and isn't it quite remarkable that both he and I happen to work at Bonanza Steakhouse and also happen to live at the Linwood Estates Apartments for Lower Income Folk.

"Remarkable," Mom says, in her I-got-a-disability-and-you-don't, superior, sarcastic voice.

I want to tell her how much I could love a guy like Douglas Moon. I go over and I put my arm buddy-like around the guy's short neck. I am tall, skin-and-bones, and he is short and clay-like in the body department. We look funny I suppose, and he looks up at me like I am being a little pushy, so I pull back.

Mom says, "I think Larry likes you Doug."

She is grinning evil. She knows I am this way for a reason.

Doug looks scared, but all my boyfriends usually do.

Doug says, "I like him too."

He looks confused.

I blush. I don't usually blush but this time I do. I picture us getting married in a wrestling ring right before a match. Gay marriage is legal in one or two states now although I don't know which. We both are dressed up in personalized, extra-shiny costumes. We both look like superstars about to beat the shit out of one another but we have to get married first.

I lean over and kiss Doug's cheek and Doug backs away and he says, "What the heck?"

He puts me in another headlock and Mom walks backwards back to her bed, saying, "Keep it down boys. I need my beauty sleep."

That happened seven months back now and Douglas Moon and me got to be fast friends, although sometimes he excludes me from his other friends, which I understand of course being who and what I am. I mean this shit is not easy. Show business is in my blood, as my mother says. My father was at one time a circus performer although she does not say with what outfit or exactly what he performed. And there are no pictures.

I like the feeling of putting on a show: shoot me.

But everyday does not usually give you major opportunities to put on a big show. So I practice hard-ass Hollywood looks whenever I can and sometimes feel the edges of my professional wrestling desire slip out of my skin into the real world like knives stabbing backwards. When I dump the garbage cans out behind Bonanza in the freezing cold I sometimes put on a big kick-ass extravaganza for myself. I huff and lift the suckers up and scream out into the night. I climb up on top of the overfilled dumpster and I jump up and down on the bags of garbage like they are the bodies of my enemies, screaming, "I am the Executioner! I am the one and the only Death-bringer-onner!"

So tonight I go into work even though I have the night off.

I have my first official murder poem, and I walk down the ice-covered hill. It's January and cold, my man, very cold. Feet on snow sounds like bones being squeezed when it gets this cold. I am wearing my coat and I have the murder poem gripped tight in my unholy hand.

When I heard last night that Douglas was joining the Army because he was tired of fucking around in this two-bit town and plus he likes guns and kicking actual ass and that whole, you know, military-like culture, I felt stunned and I thought it had to be a big joke because although my love for Douglas is not spoken out loud it is there between us like he is holding one wing of a twisting bird and I am holding the other and love would explode if we both pulled at the same time, the bird pulled apart to reveal its tiny and beating heart.

I go in through the backdoor and that redheaded kid I do not like is doing dishes. The machine is all steam and metal like a crushed submarine and the kid shoves the godforsaken racks in even though I can tell that he has not changed the water in like three hours because the dishes are coming out the opposite end covered in goo.

I do not say a word.

I am really not supposed to be here, if you want to know the truth.

I walk up to the front where Tammy, the night manager, is smoking a cigarette and talking to her boyfriend in the closed-down banquet room. She gives me her dirtiest look: "Larry what are you doing here? You are off and Dan told you not to come in if you are off."

Dan is head manager, necktie and beer-belly, and he does not like me "hanging out" here even though I told him I just come in to see if they need any help. I'm like that.

"I have something I need to drop off Tammy."

I have on a serious expression. I am acting a part. I am wounded and cold and sad from America.

"Well drop it off and leave."

Her boyfriend is a Harley-riding son of a bitch. They go back to whatever BS they were up to, and I walk up front, where people are getting prepared to close the place down, and the lights are dimmed, giving the orange booths and brown tables a haunted-house-type feel. The huge salad bar is half-taken apart, like a helicopter cannibalized for exclusive equipment.

The girl who runs cash comes across a bit scared of me. Or perhaps I am just reading into her facial expression. Perhaps she's disgusted. I just smile. I have the envelope. I am here. I turn the corner and there is Doug scraping the grill with a big steel wool brush and when he sees me he looks automatically pissed off.

"Man," he says. "I thought I told you not to come in here when I'm here, motherfucker."

It was in the bathroom last night when I told him I loved him.

I told him please do not join the Army. I had tears like insects inside my face. I got down on my knees and I yelled it. I told him I loved him. I was accidentally cross-eyed.

He said, "Get up off your fucking knees faggot."

"Do not call me that."

And he said, "That's what you are."

And I said, "It takes one to know one."

And he kicked me in the face then and my nose did bleed. I got up and got him in a headlock but he squirmed out, and then

Dan came in and he asked me to leave and I heard Doug say, "He's a big queer, Dan."

Now he throws the brush at the grill and sparks flame up.

"Make me a T-bone," I say for no reason.

"Get out of here, fruitcake," he says, and then he pushes me back toward the backdoor, and I trip and he kicks me, and sometimes when I am dreaming this is what makes me feel like he loves me, this kicking, this constant feeling being kicked in the ribs by him. A professional wrestling match in heaven.

I stand up and I say, "I got a goddamned message for you." I happen to be crying.

"What?"

He is breathing heavy and he looks at me through squinty, I-am-joining-the-goddamn-Army eyes.

I give him the envelope and I say this:

"Enjoy!"

Of course I kept a copy of the first official murder poem I gave to Doug. Here it is if it pleases the court:

> You made me cry
> Now you must die
> You curse my name
> But you are to blame
> You beat in my brains
> And the floor has got stained
> With my pretty blood and guts
> But it is you, sir, who are nuts.
>
> For my love for you is true
> The saddest part is I will have to murder you.
> I will slice your throat

Like a billy-goat
I will smash in your head
Till you, sir, are very dead
And after this thing I do
I will say I love you
And you will love me too.

"Fruitcake" happens to be his little nickname for me. As in "nuttier than."

But when one is in love like this you are Mr. Fruitcake no matter what your IQ and/or economic situation. You tend to know that there is only one thing on earth: the person you love. And you must have that person, you must bite into that love the way a grizzly bear digs into a boy scout's leg on TV. Love, this kind I have, is only three steps short of what it is that keeps you from killing the one you love. Therefore I wrote this poem in order to express this problem I have—we all have, as a nation.

Kill or be killed. Eat or be eaten.

And then Douglas is banging on my door. Mom answers it in the middle of the night, and I think from the tone of his voice he is mighty angry.

"Where is that skinny little son of a bitch?" Douglas says.

"You calm down," Mom says.

I keep listening, in my bed in the dark.

"He's threatened to kill me," Douglas says, and I think he is scared.

"What?"

"He wrote this goddamn poem here."

"Oh that. Doug, honey, Larry's not all there. He's got emotional issues. You know that."

Mom laughs and I get up and I walk into the living room, where Doug is standing in his winter coat. He is pale and his hair is all over his head. I smell the coldness of his skin, the work sweat that has frozen into his clothes.

"Mom," I say. "Leave us alone."

Mom turns around, "He is not your boyfriend. Quit writing poems." She just shakes her head and goes into her room.

I look straight at Douglas and Douglas returns the favor.

"What did you think of my poem?"

I smile, even though I am really hurting. I keep picturing him in the Army getting killed, somewhere in the sandy desert or in the hot-monkey-filled jungle. His body strung up in a tree, hanging there, his face soft as a baby's in a hospital crib.

"It's fucking shit," he says.

Douglas marches over to me and I reach out to him. He tries to pull away, but I grab him. This sudden burst of strength comes from knowing I will never get exactly what I want until things change completely, until I myself am murdered somehow. Life is about that one challenge, staying alive when what you want is never there. So I grab hold of him tighter. I feel his muscles pinned back against his bones. I am strangulating him friends. He kicks me in the stomach and I land on the floor. That kick was the hardest one I have ever felt in my whole life.

I am looking up at him. He is shining like the astronaut I know he will be. He is shining and in my pain I see that he has stopped, and when he bends down to the floor where I am suffering he is smiling.

"You want me, motherfucker?" he whispers. "You like boys?"

He is taking his shirt off, and in his underwear he stands as lonely as someone who doesn't have anybody to fight anymore.

"Come on," he says. "Come and try to kill me faggot."

I stand, a little shook still, but I take off everything too. Naked, ladies and gentlemen. This is the main event, this is what is advertised on TV as "Ass-kicking Supreme," this is something a little too mature for all audiences.

Then I get the lights and I tell him we have to be quiet while we kill each other.

"Oh, I'll be quiet," he whispers.

He silently runs into me and he takes me down to the floor, and I pull at his underwear and there it is, what I have wanted, plain as a roll of quarters. A little meanness sprouts through the quiet and I hear the roar of a crowd.

I hear him whispering, "Come on, Fruitcake. Come on. You want it."

Of course I do.

He kisses me on the mouth. I smell his kiss right before it touches down. A soft tongue is at the center of my gut's pain, a sweet sad worm is inside my big fire, and then I am not here anymore.

In my ear I hear, "Poor Fruitcake. You ain't gonna kill nobody."

He jumps on my back and he spits in his hand and rubs me up good and when it goes in I feel my back kind of break and I want to get free but also appreciate the idea of not being free, and I feel him do it and in that little quiet moment I feel what I have been missing in my life. Getting my way causes me to hum and to moan into the linoleum floor.

"You like that bitch?" he whispers.

I take a deep breath right after he finishes off. I crawl out from under all gushy and pretty and satisfied. I roll over and I put my hands around his throat and if Mom hears then she hears what she hears, and I will explain this is the way they used to wrestle in Ancient Greece.

I roll on top still holding his throat and as I strangle him I feel him try to break free but somehow I am a strong son of a bitch this time. The place where we wrestle is a rock-n-roll WWF stadium and we are tiny performers in that huge ring, and I slip what I got inside him as he squirms and I am as quiet as a mouse doing this, a mouse whispering, "I love you, you no-good son of a bitch, I fucking love you, I fucking love you."

When I finally stop, when I am through, he is as limp as a scarecrow made out of plastic garbage bags for Halloween. Still breathing though. Still here.

TRAVELING,
STAYING
STILL

I always remember the night drive down to Florida that one time. My dad had a great big Chevrolet Caprice. Todd and I were thirteen, in the back seat, Mom and Dad up front. The a-c was on, so we had a blanket on us to sleep, Mom's flat thin face resting against the seat-belt shoulder-strap. Dad's bald head pointed straight at the road. Stupid loud people voicing their opinions on a talk-radio show, debating capital punishment.

The dark rolls around the car like oily water, and Todd is pretending he's in deep sleep. I have my hand on his crotch. He is way past hard, and I am so excited, just lit up like Christmas, but have to be silent. I have to keep it totally inside, which only makes me more gleeful, more alive doing it. Mom and Dad are inches away. But that only makes it better, like the more careful and quiet I have to be, the more I can feel what it is to be alive all the way.

The silence and the secret blossom like jellyfish, unfurling into their own beautiful shapes, and Todd and I are two boys in a submarine in black water with voices going away. I pull the blanket over my head, going under, smelling our bodies mixing their smells. Heat, hair, sex. My hand stays under his briefs, and eyes closed he moves to make it easier. I am inside his underwear suddenly, holding it. I start jerking him off, and I hear him tell me in a whisper to take my underwear off. I do it. Todd starts stroking me, and I wonder if Dad knows, if Mom has woken up, and I slip my head out from under the blanket and there they are. Scarecrows, the radio is blaring.

"I think, Bob, if the death penalty was a deterrent..."

The car is going 75 miles per hour.

I go back under. The joy, knowing we are going to Florida. The joy of not knowing any better. The anticipation, this feeling as we jerk each other off, trying to keep quiet, trying not to move even as we move to get at each other, the motions under the blanket the only movement in the universe.

Finally Todd comes all over my hand, and I come all over his. I smell the warm mushroom staleness of it, then lift my head out of the blanket for air. Our bodies twitch as we relax into the smooth ride of a luxury car.

Mom and Dad say nothing, oblivious. A sign outside passes in the dark, welcoming us to the lovely state of Georgia.

DEAR

ARRID

EXTRA

DRY

Dear Arrid Extra Dry:

Thank you for making this very fine product. This Anti-Perspirant and Deodorant Spray does work 24 hours, and also it does great wonders for my problems. I hope you keep this a little private but I'm overweight and I do sweat a lot which does make me smell, but when I put on your spray it works fast. I love it. Second, I get raw under my under-arms and under my stomach and other parts also. It usually does this during the summer and boy is it summer now, 90 degrees, and we don't have air-conditioning, just fans, because my grandmother thinks air-conditioning causes lung cancer.

Simply put, I do not know what I would have done without your product. I have tried many deodorants, medicines, and baby powders for my condition. I hope you keep on making this product for years to come!

My grandmother tells me not to write to you, that you do not care about your consumers, but I figure you must because you put the address on the can right there for consumers to write in. She is always telling me to stop doing things like this. To keep my mouth shut, etc. My mom, who also uses your product, has had a stroke so she is unable to write and/or speak, but let me tell you she also enjoys the feeling of being "extra-dry" and "fresh," but my grandmother does not use deodorant, just Ivory soap and that's all and sometimes she smells. We live in close quarters here. These apartments for the lower-income people are tiny. While we watch Price Is Right or whatever, and I am seated beside my grandmother, sometimes I just about gag on her smell, but your product helps me so much I don't feel as though anybody does that with me.

Gag, I mean.

Here in the complex there are a few people who I get along with, including Rita, who runs the laundry-room (she does not smell), and Terrell, a nice black gentleman who recently got out of prison and who is living with his mom who is blind because he lost his job last week. (He does not smell at all either, but I don't think he uses your product; he smells more like cologne and cigarettes, more than anything, Old Spice brand or something of that ilk.)

Terrell calls me "Fruitcake," which is kind of derogatory you might say but he does so kiddingly, and he comes over a lot because he does not have a car and I have a video-tape collection that he likes, including the best horror-movie shows, but his mom has no VCR so he watches the movies with me in the living room at night. Sometimes he asks me for money which I say I don't have but I am thinking about giving him some. Please do not tell my grandmother. She would have a big cow, as they say.

I asked Terrell last night how I smell and he smiled great big and said, "Like a pretty little flower."

Which is a testament to you, although he was also joking I know. As I said previously, I am quite overweight but make the best of it by eating whatever I want, since I am already past the point of no return, and at the store sometimes I have to ride one of those wheelchair/carts made for invalids and fat people like yours truly. This used to be embarrassing but now I get rid of any bad feeling by eating whole boxes of cookies or whole packages of lunch-meat. It is amazing how you forget how you feel with your mouth stuffed full of the food you want, and that becomes all you want so there you go.

Last night me and Terrell watched Scream 3 which I just bought at Wal-Mart for only 12.99 and my grandmother pitched a fit there in the store and I just rode my cart through the line, proudly having it scanned. I bought Scream 3 and a can of your spray's new scent, Active Sports Powder, which does an even better job on chafing.

My grandmother said, "You can't afford movies Robert! You are on disability."

And I ignored her yelling.

Terrell said one time, "You're not some everyday problem child, Fruitcake. You got something. You just a little slow baby."

And I knew I loved him from the way his voice sounded, from the way his eyes turned to slits while he watched my movies, from the way he said I smell good (using your product: again thank you), and the way his face was not about anything other than being there with me, although I knew also he was there with me because he doesn't have a car.

When I told Terrell last night during a boring spot in Scream 3 that I am writing a letter to your company, he said, "Go for it. Maybe they'll put you on TV, Fruitcake."

He meant it too.

So then we watched the rest of Scream 3, and after it went off, around two o'clock in the morning he lit up a cigarette and I told him how much I appreciated him coming over and watching movies with me because I don't really buy the movies at Wal-Mart just for myself but to share, and I also wanted to tell him that he is the sweetest person I have ever known, but then it was not a cigarette he was lighting it was marijuana, and he offered me some.

"Here you go."

I took that smoke into my lungs. I wondered automatically if my grandmother was asleep and I thought about what Mom would think even though she can't talk or move anymore, her face a silly-putty mask of grins and frowns but I love her and I help her with her hygiene, including lifting her arms up and spraying them good with your product. She had real bad high blood pressure. That's why she had a stroke so early in her life.

I felt that marijuana cigarette smoke tingle throughout my body and I wanted to say thanks to Terrell in a different way and I got up from the couch and I said to him, "Smell my underarm," like that.

And Terrell looked at me like I was crazy.

"Really," I said. "Go ahead." I lifted both arms up like victory.

But he just looked at me and he put the tip of the marijuana joint out with spit on his fingers and he said, "Great flick Fruit-cake, but I ain't gonna smell your pits okay?"

"I just wanted to show you how this stuff work."

"No thank you."

He put the marijuana joint into his pocket. Then his face kind of lit up and he told me he might be moving to Florida near Disney World if he could get some money for a bus ticket and maybe some new clothes.

"Do you know where I might be able to get some money?" He smiled. He had stringy spongy hair going bald on top. But he was well-built and I liked looking at him while he watched the movies I bought at Wal-Mart. He liked the same movies I do. It was nice to have something in common.

"You could get a job," I said.

"I've tried Fruitcake. God have I tried."

He leaned close to me. "You got any money on you? Cause if you had some money I might a strike a little deal with you baby."

Up close he smelled like a hot kitchen and that cologne mixed up, sweat and cleanness, and I took a deep breath, watching his lips go over his teeth.

I did have some of my check left, of course. As soon as it comes to me in the mail (I do not trust direct-deposit), I walk to the convenience store down at the end of the road, and cash it, and give my grandmother the rent money but the rest is mine for movie-buying plus I often buy three or four cans of your product because I tend to run out because I use it at least seven or eight times a day.

I had 100 dollars hid in my room in a small Tupperware container.

"You got some money, don't you?"

His kindness was also not so kind, I know. Please don't think I am that stupid because I am not. I knew he was kind and I knew he was also cruel but therein lies the mystery and when I nodded my head Terrell clapped his hands.

"Wanna know the little deal baby, the one I can offer you? First of all, how much you got?"

"One hundred," I said, and I was feeling shaky, and I knew something was going to happen.

"Well for that Fruitcake I will let you have some of this," he said.

He pointed down at his privates, and held his privates through his pants, and I looked away, but then I looked back and I looked into his face and he was being kind not cruel then.

I stopped in the bathroom. I sprayed my arm pits and the place under my belly and behind my knees and all over my privates. In the mirror as I sprayed I looked as big as an octopus that had somehow escape the zoo. I was whiter than a peeled potato, and my glasses were crooked, and my hair was oily. I sprayed more on of your product. I felt fresher and fresher, and on my way back I stopped off and opened the door to my mom and grandmother's room. They sleep in the same big bead. My mom's eyes were wide open because this is the way she sleeps now. And my grandmother was snoring big-time and if she knew what was about to happen in her apartment she would have a stroke too. First she does not like black people that much. Second she does not like queers.

I got the money. Then I said, "Let's go to my bedroom."

Terrell laughed. "You the man."

In my room I said I would like to see him nude and he said he would like to see the 100 dollars and I said look and he saw it and he stripped for me. I know without the money this would not ever have happened no matter how good I smelled but somehow I pretended he was loving me back, and like the food I eat to forget that I eat too much, I felt a love come from him that was the love I was giving him and he did love me while he stripped, his face shining in the light of my bedroom, with the empty cans of your product decorating shelves like a History of Arrid Extra Dry Museum.

When Terrell was naked I thought I might not be able to talk, but I said, "You are so beautiful."

"Thank you," he said in a whisper.

It was over way too soon.

He put his clothes back on and he lit up the joint and he asked me to turn the one light I had on off. He opened the window to let the smoke out. My grandmother has told me repeatedly that my mom dropped me on a concrete driveway when I was one year old and this is why I am this way. She said my mom was in a hurry to watch some show on TV and she got out of the car with me in her arms and she tripped and little me fell on my head and sometimes in dreams I remember this fall. I remember the smack of concrete against my skull like the hand of God telling me: notice things. I remember seeing stars the size of Cadillacs riding past my crib and the pain was not pain it was more like wallpaper coming off a wall.

Terrell gave me this marijuana joint and I took in the illegal smoke and he said, "I guess I am gonna have to go Fruitcake. You did good buddy."

He patted my head and I wanted to hate him, but his kindness, even with money involved like this which is not right I know, was too much, and I told him he was beautiful again, and I said, "Why don't you, just once, smell my armpit here? See how good this stuff works?"

He looked almost mad then. Like he really wanted to leave. But he leaned down and I lifted my arm, and he said, after taking a big whiff, "That is some good deodorant Fruitcake. That stuff surely does work my friend."

In many ways, your Arrid Extra Dry is a godsend.

It has given me the confidence to go on. I know that I don't smell, and that is one less worry to carry around on my journey through life. The doctors I have seen have told my grandmother I have social problems due to my situation. Sometimes I cannot shut my mouth. Sometimes I don't know when to say no to myself. There is no pill for this, say the doctors. However, there is a remedy for my body odor. Your product. Thank you, thank you, thank you. I cannot say that enough.

In conclusion, I hope you never stop making this wonderful product. Thank you so very much for reading this letter, and I look forward to hearing from you.

Yours truly,

AFTER
SCHOOL

In 1983, when I was about to graduate high school, Kelson was one of the most popular kids in our class. Sun-tanned from playing on the tennis team, he wore pastel Izods with the collars turned up and had perfectly styled blonde hair. He drove to school in his mom's beige Cadillac.

I didn't understand why he gave me the time of day, but suddenly there he would be in the hall next to me, chatting in that sarcastic but over-friendly manner of his. With him I always swayed between total humiliation and wondering if he was actually interested in what I had to say. I was Kelson's opposite: a pudgy, white-trash kid who liked to draw pretend album covers and had a C- average.

Kelson's parents were upstanding small-business people. He was their oldest, a shining example of upward mobility in a small town, and unbeknownst to them a great big hungry faggot. We'd met at the high-school radio station when we were sophomores. He was already the big cheese there, doing a sports show. One day, when I was getting ready to sign on for a shift and he was waiting to do his sports-show promo, we got into a conversation about Talking Heads and David Bowie. He was so impressed I knew who the Ramones were that he patted me on the back like we were smoking cigars in a drawing room.

Eventually conversations at the radio station turned into going out for pizza some nights, or to the movies but never as a part of any group. That way we could talk about cute guys, and he could tell me how he had sucked off a fellow tennis player in the backseat of his mom's car. At the time, I had my own secret boyfriend, some doofus who would butt-fuck me during sleepovers and pretend it was some kind of hypnosis.

Kelson was the homecoming king. After we graduated (me barely, him top of the class), Kelson traveled to Miami for an extended vacation all by himself. In August, he came back with

Archie. They were staying at some guy's apartment downtown because Kelson's mom wouldn't let Archie and him stay there together. In Miami, Kelson had gone full-tilt homosexual. He called me one night and invited me over.

When I got there, Archie and Kelson were in the bathroom fucking. Roger, the fat, bald, middle-aged guy whose place it was, was smoking pot and eating a ham sandwich. Roger was a deejay at a local radio station Kelson had met while interning there. He was closeted and gay and obviously in love with Kelson, but that meant being used by Kelson. MTV flickered on the TV. Roger told me that Archie and Kelson had been fucking since Kelson called me.

"They took a can of Crisco in there," he said, laughing, almost pissed but doped up enough to get the joke. "I shit you not."

I sat there with Roger and watched Taco sing "Puttin' on the Ritz." We could hear Kelson moaning above the techno sadness. A half-hour later Archie and Kelson came out of the bathroom, dewy from their shower, the soap smell and heat filling the whole apartment. Archie was even more beautiful than Kelson, tall and lean and tan with long black hair and thick lips. He wore a pair of shorts and nothing else. Kelson was in jeans and a t-shirt, barefooted.

"Banner!" Kelson said. "Lookie here, it's Banner!"

He was so ecstatically alive it was scary. Archie was rolling his eyes. He didn't even want to be introduced to me. He sat down on a chair adjacent to Roger, displaying the nonchalance of someone who didn't speak the language and had no desire to learn it, as if just existing in the same universe as a ham sandwich was beneath him.

"Hey Banner, this is Archie. He is my homosexual lover. Fuck everybody, I'm out and proud," Kelson said. Even though what he proclaimed seemed rote, his voice had a thunderbolt inside it as he said it. He came over and shook my hand like an overexcited businessman.

"Isn't Archie beautiful?" Kelson said even more loudly.

Archie said, "Shut up, Kelson."

You could tell Kelson was trying to find an equilibrium with Archie—a beautiful fag from Miami agonizing in this apartment. Kelson seemed even more attractive to me now, but I just sat there, quiet, taking it all in. I wanted them to want me to join them in the bathroom the next time they did anything, but I choked down that desire before it could pass over into the outside world. I knew I was just what Kelson wanted me to be: a witness to his bravado and nothing more. I simply had the privilege of basking in his glow.

Kelson ran over to Archie and tried to tongue-kiss him and Archie said, "Get off me, you fucking idiot." His voice was a prissy blast of steam.

They went back into the bathroom a few minutes later, and that was that. I drove home with the two of them still going at it.

I didn't see Kelson again until December that year. Roger was having a Christmas party, and Kelson said he'd give me a ride. I was standing outside the house waiting. It was halfway snowing, a little after nightfall. I had a bad sore throat and had almost called to cancel but couldn't. I wanted to see him too badly.

When he pulled up in his mom's Cadillac, he was playing Missing Persons on the stereo.

"Banner. Banner!" he yelled as soon as I got in. "What do you say?"

"What?" I asked.

"You know what." He looked at me like a drill sergeant.

"Pizza and beer," I said.

"Fuck yes!" he yelled as we pulled out.

By then, my secret high-school boyfriend had told me he was not gay and that I sickened him. He'd gone off to Purdue University. I'd gone to art school and met some people, mostly sad bohemian losers who had to work at fast-food restaurants to pay for their art supplies like I did. But I was always a little backwards, even with my own kind. So that night I felt totally in love with Kelson, violently so. Maybe it was the sore throat or my dad leaving my mom or just life in general, but I knew that night was the last chance I might have. I kept popping mentholated cough drops, the red ones that taste almost like cherry and almost like gasoline.

"How's Archie?" I asked.

Kelson didn't say anything. At a stoplight he finally said, laughing, "He left me. So now my mom is letting me drive her car again."

Roger's party had only two other people at it, his fat, balding-like-him sister and her skinny husband. Kelson and I sat together on the couch. I drank a lot. I also kept popping cough drops. The mix of the Jack and the cherry-menthol was soothing my throat, but then it all started to get gassy and blurry with the pot and the pizza and Kelson's breathy comments mixed in. I laughed too much, a fake-laugh I used to conceal how sick and love-sick I was feeling.

We left a little while later. Kelson wanted to drive to Indianapolis to go to some gay bar he'd been to. I was elated, feverish, and very, very drunk. Once we got onto the interstate, I turned the stereo off and I told him.

I told him I wanted to suck him off, in a drunken slur. Humiliation and desire were intermingling into a warm and horrible trance.

Kelson didn't look at me. I think his uncharacteristic silence was an attempt to be kind. Right after saying it, I had to puke. He pulled the car over. I got out, gagging and sobbing. I puked for what seemed like hours. When I got back in, we didn't say one word to each other. He got off at the next exit and took me home.

The next time I saw Kelson was eight years later, 1991. I was living in Indianapolis with Bill, the guy I would end up with. It was late summer. We had walked downtown to get something to eat. There was a concert going on in the park so we sat on a bench to listen. Then I heard that unmistakable voice.

"Banner!"

I turned around and Kelson was sitting at the side of a marble fountain. Zydeco music spilled out of staticky speakers. He was very thin, his hair not as blonde, dressed in khakis and a short-sleeved dress shirt with a clip-on necktie. He ran to us. I introduced him to Bill, and he shook hands with both of us.

"So how are you doing, Banner? Remember I always called you that?"

He laughed and the meanness that I remembered inside the laugh was all gone, as if surgically removed. The clip-on and the khakis looked like a joke, but the overly sincere look in his eyes said no. He was a scarecrow version of himself.

Kelson looked at Bill and grinned. "So he's your boyfriend, right?"

"Yeah," I said.

Bill laughed. I'd talked to him about Kelson before, describing how desperate and stupid I was in high school, how Kelson was the most popular boy in school and me the least popular and how we had been connected to each other by destiny.

Now there was nothing to say, but Kelson kept on talking about his insurance business, about how he had been living in Miami for a while but then he decided to come back to town because it was hard for him to make a living partying so much.

THIS IS TRUE LOVE

Each sentence was punctuated by a creepy, apologetic laugh. Finally, I said Bill and I needed to get back home. Kelson offered to drive us in his Buick. We accepted. It just seemed easier.

It was obvious he was living out of his car. Piles of clothes in the backseat, a plastic bag of toiletries on the back floor. Lots of pill bottles in there, too. We all sat up front. As he drove, Kelson talked more about where life had taken him.

"I'm in between homes right now. I was living with my mom, but things got you know tense there."

His fingers trembled so badly around the steering wheel that he had to make himself loosen his grip every few seconds.

Bill and I were renting a dilapidated Victorian house, and when we got there, Kelson told us how great the house was, even though it looked like shit inside and out. We hung out on the porch. I was smoking then and Kelson gave me a lecture about how bad it was not just for me, but for Bill.

"Second-hand smoke is a killer," he said, all serious.

Then he asked if he could stay the night with us. He tried to say it with sexy vibrato.

"I mean, just a couple of days and then I'll find a place. Maybe we could share the bed, huh? What do you think, Banner? A little threesome?"

Bill and I looked at each other in the way that people witnessing tragedies do.

It was shocking, but I had this sense that this was his life now. It was old hat, and you can take him up on it or not it didn't matter to him. He just needed a place to sleep, and if he had to pull a threesome, that was cool. It was gruesome to watch, but I felt more connected to him in that moment than I ever had in high school. All I had ever felt for Kelson went from obsession to sympathy.

Kelson had no other options. He had lost the most vital part of himself somewhere along the way. And now he was totally alone. But the sympathy was evaporating even as it formed.

"Yeah," I said. "We really are into threesomes. Can't get enough threesomes."

Bill laughed, "It's all we do on weekends. Threesome Central right here."

Part of it was AIDS, but he didn't tell us that. I found out a few years later. His mom finally let him come back home when he was about to die, and he died in the bedroom he grew up in. They had a funeral, but no one other than the family was invited.

That night I don't think Bill and I were afraid of the specter of AIDS as much as Kelson's need to be near us. It was like he had skidded into a new kind of loneliness, and that was all that was left of him, a loneliness you just can't be a part of if you want to stay sane.

Bill and I made something up about how the guy we rented the house from didn't want us to have guests. He'd had a really rotten tenant before. He was always in and out checking on things.

"Oh, yeah, I understand," Kelson said.

He looked me right in the eye, and I think, at least I hope, he did understand. He grinned at me, not a smile as much as a secret prayer. Then he asked to use the phone. We heard him talk to someone (his mom) about tonight and how he was a little sick of this treatment and how he was sorry he was such a goddamn disappointment. The conversation went on for a while. Bill and I stayed in the kitchen and tried not to hear the rest of it.

When he left, Kelson was okay, or close to okay. We had some beers on the porch. He got nostalgic. He talked about being on the tennis team. He even talked about Archie, how beautiful Archie had been, and about Miami in the early eighties. Kelson stopped talking then, as if he needed all his concentration to get out of his hole of regret. He looked at his hands in the porch light. He held them out and they were shaking.

"That'll stop in a few seconds."

He held out his shaking hands and stared at them like a wizard. We stared at them too. It was like he was trying to stop everything by staring his hands into submission. And the shaking stopped soon thereafter. He smiled at us.

"Mind over matter," he half-whispered, then let out a big laugh.

What kept sticking in my mind was a memory from 1983, when David Bowie's album Let's Dance came out. I had lied to Kelson and told him I had the album, that I was the first person to have it.

He asked to borrow it.

He had money. He could have just gone out and bought it himself. But I think he suspected I was lying to impress him, so he pushed it.

"Sure," I said, knowing I'd have to wait until I had my paycheck to buy it.

On Monday I took the album to school. Finally, I saw Kelson at the end of the day, by a water fountain near the gym's back door. I ran to him, showing him the album.

He just looked at me, a beautiful snarl encased in Plexiglas inside his eyes.

"Oh, I went ahead and bought it. Thanks anyway," he said.

Then he walked out to his mom's Cadillac in the parking lot. I stood there holding the album, watching him pull out of his parking space. I couldn't stop watching.

DON'T

MIND

IF

I

DO

The Wednesday night before, Angie and her next-door neighbor Rocky buy Thanksgiving groceries. At the end of the haul, standing at the register, Angie witnesses the tally: $409.42. Rocky's paying for it all.

"Jesus," she whispers. The little teenaged guy bagging everything is working hard to keep up.

Rocky says, "I like doing it up right."

Dressed in one of those dark blue track suits he's always wearing, his salt-and-pepper hair combed back, Rocky takes out his wallet, pulls a credit card out, swipes.

Soon the kid gets way behind, so Angie and Rocky start bagging up stuff as well.

"I think you are in a manic phase or something," Angie says, laughing.

"Probably," Rocky says back.

They are always joking around.

Once everything is loaded up, Rocky drives them back to Deerfield Estates. Angie's house, and the house Rocky shares with his partner Larry, are the only occupied ones now (other than three at the very back end) in this part of the development, about 45 minutes outside of Atlanta. The other houses, big stony mini-mansions all built in the same couple years, have been mostly foreclosed on. Her house is about to go under too. That last payment was a loan from Rocky.

A few years back, the bank people talked like her job managing an Applebee's, plus her then husband's job selling cars, would do just fine. Not explaining of course how the whole situation would work out, as in they would start out paying a small mortgage payment but a couple years in, the payments would quadruple. She just went with it. She wanted it so badly.

They even took out an extra loan to buy furniture which was just folded into the mortgage itself.

Now it's Thanksgiving three years later. She's still working at Applebee's and the furniture still looks great, so does the house, don't get her wrong, but there are realty signs in almost every yard here. Every other week a bunch of guys in green overalls mow all the lawns, the realtors trying to keep ahead of any semblance of abandonment.

Rocky and Larry, though, have their house completely paid for, even if what they paid is now only a fraction of what it's worth. Their house is the prettiest one in the neighborhood too, right at the back of the cul-de-sac, with awnings and a stone path and beautiful landscaping leading up to the front door.

Rocky pulls into his driveway now, and the garage door goes up. They take in the groceries and put everything up in the kitchen. Larry used to cook all the time before the brain tumor. He was executive chef at the restaurant he and Rocky owned until they sold it a few years back. They've been together for almost 29 years.

Halfway through getting everything put away, they hear Larry yelling from the basement.

"The master beckons," Rocky says.

Angie laughs and follows behind him, down the carpeted stairs to the basement. It's furnished with leather upholstered couch and chairs, chunky wood coffee and end tables, a big TV bolted to the wall that's on with the local news, the only light, and right in front of that, in his big recliner, Larry is holding his Big Gulp cup. A skinny little man in sweatpants and a sweatshirt and a panama hat he always wears. Connie their fat cat is over by one of the bar stools, licking her butt with her back paws up in the air.

"Honey," Rocky says. "We are right here. What are you going all the way blind now?"

Larry stops yelling and says, "I can see fine."

They moved Larry down here after his last big surgery because he was having to use a walker and the stairs are a total bitch.

"I see you've hydrated yourself," Rocky says, looking into the Big Gulp cup Larry drinks from. He has a thing for white wine.

Larry ignores, looks at Angie, smiles. His face has a melted innocence to it. Rocky told her the first time they knew something was wrong, they were at a Winona Judd concert in Chattanooga, Tennessee, a big outdoor festival. They were running to get to their seats, and Larry just suddenly collapsed on the blacktop, people running past. Rocky started to laugh and he noticed this stricken look on Larry's face, a defeated expression he had never seen before on anyone's face. Larry was only 44 then. He could not get up off the ground. He was seeing flashing lights and he could not move his legs.

Larry says, "Turkey Day tomorrow."

"We're gonna eat like stinking pigs Larry," Angie says, flopping down on the sofa.

"You all get those little marshmallows?"

"Yes," Rocky says. "And four gallons of Chardonnay."

"And everything else in the store," Angie says.

Larry laughs, but then the laugh kind of fades.

"Guess who I saw over there?" he says, pointing to the sliding glass basement doors that lead out to a little patio area.

"Who?" Angie says.

Rocky takes Larry's empty Big Gulp and goes over to the paneled bar, gets the big bottle of Chardonnay out, pours.

"Troy."

Troy is Angie's ex.

"You sure?" Angie says.

"He just came up to the sliding glass and looked in and I waved and he yelled and asked where you were and I said I forgot."

"Where'd he go?"

Larry loses it for a second, like an airplane just took off inside his head and sucked away all the air and thought in its ascension. Rocky brings back the replenished Big Gulp. Puts it in Larry's hand. It has a big red lid and red straw on top. Larry takes a long sip from the straw.

Angie looks through the sliding glass windows. You can see part of the front of her house from this vantage point. She can see Troy's old blue Chevy truck in her driveway.

"He's over there," she says.

The Big Gulp starts to shake. Rocky carefully takes it from Larry's hand and puts in on the end table next to the recliner.

Larry says, "I just need a little nap."

"Go ahead honey," Rocky says, taking Larry's panama hat off. Larry has a full head of lovely sandy brown hair, except for the left side where they had shaved for the surgery. It's been growing back in a weird and weedy way around his ear.

"Don't mind if I do," he says with his eye closed.

Troy's in her kitchen sitting at her table in an old red t-shirt and blue jeans and sneakers. He smiles as soon as he sees her.

"Hello Starshine," he says.

"I thought you were going to spend the holidays with your mom and dad."

"We got into it. They asked me to leave. So on, so forth."

He laughs, and then the laugh slows down to a slight smile, almost a smirk.

"Fuck it," she says.

"Fuck what?"

"Take a big long look at this place, okay?"

She grabs his arm and it's cold and has a ropy feel. She pulls him into the living room, hallway, up the stairs to the bedrooms, each room furnished with the glossy furniture that will be repossessed too.

"What?" he says, laughing.

"We're getting foreclosed on finally. It's over. Not that you give a shit of course, but still."

They are in the master bedroom. Cream-colored carpet, the beige bedspread, floral pillows, that big painting of a beach and clouds they got at the furniture store.

"Nothing we can do?" he says.

She wants to slap his fucking boyish face.

"Where have you been?"

"Staying with mom and dad. The thought of going back to the rehab place is just stupid. I was clean for like a month. Swear to God. But then I just went for it."

He grins, the grin he used to use when he was thirty pounds heavier and dressed in a short-sleeved dress-shirt and clip-on neck-tie, downing a breakfast shake on the way out to car lot.

"I thought why in the hell am I going through all this shit when all I need is you?"

They wind up in the bed. He can't get hard at first but then it happens and he doesn't say anything after that, just goes into those noises she remembers, growls and grunts and laughs. After they do it, he's almost warm next to her and he talks about how his mom and dad don't know what to do with him, and he was thinking maybe they could turn this whole thing around here, renegotiate the loan or whatever the fuck. Aren't there government programs to help people get out of this shit? Can't they sue those goddamned predatory bank-people?

For some reason she starts thinking about Thanksgiving tomorrow. She envisions the food Rocky bought, all of them feasting tomorrow afternoon, and then maybe Larry, if he's okay, and Rocky, and Troy and she will play Monopoly, one of Larry's favorites, everyone getting drunk and just disappearing into the holiday like that. She has to work Black Friday, the evening shift – her Applebee's is right outside a big shopping center so it will be a fucking madhouse.

She looks over at Troy.

"Shut up," she whispers, even though he isn't talking.

"I'm sorry."

"Let's forget it," she whispers. "Let's not talk about anything else okay?"

"I like that. Yeah. Sure. I like not saying anything else."

He kisses her. She closes her eyes.

All the horrible shit he's done to her. Getting a credit card in her name. Taking off in her car and abandoning it that one time when he got out to buy drugs and got high after buying them and couldn't remember where he parked it and so on so forth. What really hurts the most is what he used to be. That character now in her head, when she first met him at the Applebee's a few years back. She assistant-manages the place now, but back then she was bartender and he'd come in after he got off work at Jeff Rogers Cadillac, flushed and full of life and just hang there, drinking whatever drinks she made him, always telling her to surprise him, a different clip-on necktie every night. She'd whip up some fantastic concoctions and he would just go on and on about how fucking great each cocktail was.

Thanksgiving morning, she makes pancakes. Troy comes down and flops on the sofa, turns on the TV with the remote. It's the parade.

"What time we gonna go over to Larry and Rocky's?" he says. He isn't wearing a shirt, and his hair is tangled from sleep. The ribs inside his chest look like fingers inside a tight pocket.

"Around one. Rocky is gonna get the turkey going."

She sets the table. Warms the syrup. Gets it all laid out on the table.

"You think I can take a shower? I brought some clothes," he says, looking up from his plate.

"Sure. Help yourself."

He gets up and goes out to his truck and comes back with a duffel-bag and goes upstairs. She goes up a couple minutes later. She can hear the shower going. The bathroom door is closed, but she needs to get her toothbrush so she pushes on it, and there he is on the toilet, in his tidy-whities, shooting up. He doesn't even jump or notice she's there. He just continues, and the heat of the shower rushes into her eyes, across her face. He looks up at her, out of it, even while he's continuing to push in on the syringe. He pulls it out and folds his arm up against any blood that might seep out. He's got it down. He falls back a little on the toilet. Just there, doing that.

A few hours later they walk over to Rocky and Larry's. It's gloomy but warm, a mist clinging to the pine trees and bushes and roofs. Troy is in a blue flannel shirt and new jeans. He walks next to her, smelling like the soap she uses.

"This is gonna rock," he says, as he walks toward the sliding glass doors. His voice has a nasty dreaminess to it from the drug, almost like he's talking in a porn movie. He's upbeat and dead at the same time.

Troy opens the sliding glass entrance to the basement.

"Get your hind-ends in here," Larry says.

Larry's in his lounger with Connie on his lap, the panama hat cockeyed on his head. You can smell a warm turkey-fog even down here.

"Larry how's it hanging bud?" Troy asks.

"Great." Larry's eyes are half-closed, and then he widens them. "Good to see you Troy."

The four of them, back when Troy lived here those few months, would meet up for card games and movie nights, and she could tell even then Larry had a crush on Troy. Troy knew too and he didn't care. Now that Larry is worse it seems like the crush has enlarged with the same stubbornness as the tumor. He stares at Troy as Troy walks over to him, and then Larry puts his arms up, Connie jumping down. Troy leans in and Larry grabs onto him tight.

Angie goes up to the kitchen. Rocky has actually gotten everything ready already. Turkey, ham, yams, rolls, corn, mashed potatoes, two kinds of stuffing, gravy, broccoli salad, cauliflower casserole, and so on.

"Jesus Christ Rocky," she says.

He laughs, coming from behind the open fridge door with a bowl of grapes.

"I got started as soon as you left last night and I just went for it. And then I got up real early this morning too," he says.

So alive right now, so pink-skinned and healthy, his eyes glittering.

Angie and Rocky make plates and deliver them to Troy and Larry, who are now chatting in the basement. Troy's eyes are like busted glass.

Once they all get situated with their food, Rocky puts on a Carrie Underwood CD Larry likes on the stereo, turned low, lights some candles.

"Larry? Honey? Don't you want to eat?" Rocky says.

Larry doesn't open his eyes, his plate on an end-table now. He starts to shake a little, and his arms stiffen so that they go up and down as if he's imitating a robot.

"It's a seizure," Rocky says. "He's been having them lately. Real mild ones like that. The doctor said there's nothing to do but have him ride them out like this. They've given him anti-seizure meds but they just seem to lessen the time of them."

Troy puts his plate on the coffee-table and stands.

"Your bathroom is over there, right?"

"Yup. Right next to where we got the table out."

Troy walks into the bathroom. Carrie Underwood's voice is a high-pitch trill like some lonely bird call in an empty parking lot after you get off work. Larry's arms have flattened next to him, his face blank, and for a minute she wants to get the hell out of there.

Rocky says, "It's like he's riding a rollercoaster inside his head, you know? And right now it looks like the ride's about to stop. He'll wake in a few, hungry as all get out."

Rocky leans in and pulls a piece of white meat from a platter and takes a bite. Smiles.

Troy walks out of the bathroom, flushed and fidgety and too happy for it not to be more heroin. He's doing too much. He'll OD. Troy relaxes into the cushions until it seems like he might have a seizure too. He breathes heavily and then pops up, all smiles, grabs his food, looks at it and puts it back on the coffee-table.

"You okay?" Angie asks.

He nods.

"Yeah." His eyes close too slowly, then open themselves too wide. "Sure."

She looks at Rocky. Rocky knows. This has happened before, Troy getting high and trying to make it seem normal and when that used to happen she would get infuriated, kick him out, make a big scene out of it.

Larry's eyes open. He looks around the room.

"Hey Larry. You hungry now hon?"

Larry can't talk for a minute, but then he nods. Rocky helps him with the plate of food. Larry starts to eat, slowly spooning stuffing into his mouth, then stopping, looking around.

Troy drifts off, sliding back into the couch, his Thanksgiving uneaten.

Angie and Rocky get tickled. There's a feeling between the two of them she can't really put into words, a sudden realization of the slow absurdity of the day, really of life itself.

"You think Larry will want anymore?" Angie asks, laughing a little bit still.

"No. It'll take him all afternoon to finish what I gave him," Rocky says.

"I don't think Troy's going to be eating anything."

Rocky looks up from putting some tinfoil around the white meat, whispering, "Is he super-high or what?"

Angie nods and laughs some more.

"What a magical holiday we're having," Rocky whispers.

They used to joke about all the other losers in the neighborhood, since Rocky and Larry were like the sanest homeowners on the block. The disability insurance they had. The good investments Rocky made with the money they got for the restaurant. When she asked him to borrow that last mortgage payment, it was like she was admitting she wasn't in his league anymore, but he was so kind and easygoing about it she couldn't hate him for having what she didn't.

Rocky and Angie start taking some of the dishes back up to the kitchen. Rocky starts washing the pots he used. Angie rinses and dries. After they finish what they can, Rocky opens the freezer door, grabs a fresh pack of Salem Lights and says, "I'm smoking again."

"Can I bum one?"

They go out on the front porch. Deerfield Estates is misty-gray and calm, all those empty houses around them regal like monuments.

"Are you okay?" Angie asks Rocky. He's quietly sucking in smoke near the edge of the porch.

"Yes," he says. "Just exhausted." He tries to laugh.

Angie breathes in the smoke, closes her eyes. She's floating for a few seconds.

"Sometimes," Rocky says, "I just wish it was over. But then as soon as I wish that I want to shoot myself for thinking it."

He sucks in smoke dramatically, and then comes over to her, throwing his cigarette onto the ground.

"You need me to write you another check?" he asks.

"Don't worry about it."

"What if you moved in here with me and Larry? You could help out. Rent-free. You know? Just let the house go? Sometimes I'll think I wish me and Larry would have never bought this place. Back when we did, it was flourishing here you know? We were the first ones to get in on a good thing, we thought. And now it's just this. You never know, do you? But I do need help sometimes."

Angie can't think of anything to say, to fill in the gap between what he's offered and what she's feeling. He wants her to hold him, so she does, and for a second she knows she can count on him for anything, knows he will help her no matter what she needs, but then that somehow just pisses her off.

Troy and Larry are both asleep downstairs now.

Rocky and Angie go back in and do more dishes. She tells Rocky she needs to go to the bathroom, so she goes to the one connected to Rocky's bedroom down the hall from the kitchen. She walks through his bedroom, stands in front of his bed for a second. It's a king-sized bed he used to share with Larry, with a bunch of pillows, a satiny maroon cover, a dark-wood headstand. There's a large dark-wood wardrobe, a couple of antique lamps. She doesn't know exactly what she's doing, but there's a feeling that she needs to be doing this. She's looking for something right then she can't really let herself know about. Then her eyes catch on a pile of keys and change on his dresser by the bathroom door. She sees his wallet.

She takes the gold one, the American Express. She shoves it into her pocket, doesn't go to the bathroom, and walks back to the kitchen to help Rocky finish up.

Back at the house, Troy collapses on the bed up in her room, drifts off. She puts the credit card she stole from Rocky into her purse. Troy twitches a little, rolling over and back on his back. His cheeks sink in as he snores, little bird-like reminders of how much weight he's lost, how maybe toothlessness just might be on the horizon.

"Wake up," she says, putting the shit up. "Wake up!"

Troy does not stir. He just keeps breathing. She wonders if she should take him to the ER, or he needs fucking Narcan or whatever, but right then he opens his eyes wide and he looks at her and he says he's sorry but he's relaxing. He thanks her for letting him relax. He smiles at her and then slides back into his abyss.

She gets up and goes over to her purse and pulls the credit card out. Her blood makes a noise in her head, a scary buzz, and for a second of two she truly wishes she could join Troy in his abyss, just slide right into it, but then she stomps down the stairs, out her front door.

Angie knocks really hard and rings the doorbell at Rocky and Larry's. There's no answer. She pounds on the door for a little while longer, thinking about how she'll give the goddamn credit card back and tell Rocky she's sorry, she's just losing her shit, and Rocky will probably not know what to do, or maybe he'll laugh it off, or tell her to go straight to hell, or even call the cops, or maybe he will forgive her right off. A stupid act of desperation, a call for help. Whatever you call it.

Still no answer.

Angie walks back behind their house, to the sliding glass doors. They're not locked. She slides them open, turns on the basement lights.

Larry is not in his lounger, not on the couch that makes a bed. Maybe Larry had a seizure that scared Rocky into calling the EMTs, or maybe Larry has died, or...

She walks up the stairs.

Larry is at the kitchen table, his panama hat covering his eyes. On the table is all the leftover food from earlier, unwrapped from the plastic Rocky and she had put over it all. Bowls and plates and tinfoil pans of turkey and ham, potatoes, macaroni and cheese, pie, all of it, and Larry with a spoon, getting ready to put a large quantity of a mix of almost everything into his mouth.

"Larry?"

He just puts the food in his mouth and chomps on it, looking away from her, then back.

"Larry? Where's Rocky?"

He eats slowly, swallowing finally, and then says, "Out."

"Where?"

Larry finishes swallowing it all.

"Whoring around."

Larry laughs. He is not mad or upset, just completely hungry and solidly committed to getting over being hungry.

"What?"

"He goes out at night to get him some sometimes. The nurse's aide didn't show up like she said she would but he said he'd be back in a few hours and I said okay."

Angie walks over to the table and sits down.

"How did you get up here?"

Larry takes the spoon and dips it into a big bowl of cranberry sauce.

"I can walk if I need to. Those steps, up here. If I need to. Wore me out. I went to sleep, and then I woke up and I was starving and I knew Rocky had took off. He goes out at night to whore around sometimes. We joke about it. I don't want to have anything to do with that. I don't feel like it."

He eats the cranberry sauce. He dips the big spoon into a dish of cream corn. Eats that.

"You want anything?" he asks.

Angie stands up. She takes the credit card out of her jean pocket. She puts it on the countertop next to the coffeemaker.

"No thanks."

She sits with Larry for a little while, watching him eat. She gets a washcloth to wipe his face after he's done. As she wipes it all off, she feels the loose skin around his jaw and neck. The way his head almost wants to fall back from his neck, it's so heavy, but then she realizes he's still hungry. He eats a little more.

Once he's totally done, she puts the food back for him. Larry belches quietly. He laughs at himself.

"I'm tired again," he says.

"You need help back downstairs?"

He looks at her. She remembers when she first met Larry. He had the brain tumor back then, but he could walk okay, they were trying chemo and other stuff. He looked handsome back then, even handsomer than Rocky. She remembers how they both came over when she and Troy first moved in. They brought over banana bread in an elaborate gift basket, with some packets of flower seeds, a collection of little votive candles, bubble-bath. She remembers how meeting them that first time was kind of like her way into a new life. Just like buying the house, like she was in a different zone, one that would allow her escape from what she thought her life would always be.

"I need help," Larry says.

She helps him up. He's heavy against her, walking toward the stairs. On the way down she feels like he might fall on top of her.

In the basement she helps him into his lounger. Connie comes out from behind the bar, automatically climbing up into his lap. Angie grabs a throw from the couch and spreads it over both of them. Larry conks out right away, breathing deeply. When Angie gets ready to go, she turns back around and looks at him. She can see that this time it just might not be a seizure, and it might not be sleep. He's completely still, the cat jumping away.

He's happy, she thinks. Or at least that's what it seems like right then, like happiness has taken him over for good.

ANYONE
CAN
SEE

1

Three of Danny's friends come into Halloween City mid-afternoon. Two with glossy shaved heads, one with a red crew-cut. The lead guy has the crew-cut. As soon as he walks in, he replaces his sunglasses carefully with super-stylish horn-rimmed glasses. He sneaks up behind Danny and says "Boo!"

"Fuck you Nolan," Danny says, but he's laughing.

"You are on your way to great things here Danny," Nolan shoots back.

"Please shut up."

There aren't that many customers, so besides me there's just one other cashier, who is also the manager. She's on her break. Until these three showed up it had been just Danny and me in the store, and some guy in back unloading stock. Me standing upfront at my register watching him unpacking plastic vampire-teeth, shooting each one in its little cellophane sack with a price gun.

Danny turns back to his price-gunning now. He is more beautiful than they are, taller and built better, with the chiseled features of an old-time movie-star nobody talks about anymore.

"We're getting spooky shit for my party," Nolan says.

He walks around Danny looking at the shelves filled with costumes and props. Right now, the old Staples building Halloween City occupies is overflowing with cut-rate merchandise, other crap still in huge cardboard boxes all around the store.

"Can you get us a discount?"

"Don't think so."

The other two guys say some other things about Danny's loser status, laughing like it's just a part of the game they always play.

I am close but at an angle at the checkout, leaning on the counter next to the register, my leg twitching a little. The manager says I can use a stool but I choose to stand for most of the shift. I turn away from looking at them for a second and check out the bright blue October sky outside. It is one of those chilly extra-shiny days, when empty parking lots look like everything you've ever forgotten. I can hear the four of them talk and laugh and then get quiet and then some more laughs on the other side of the store as they walk through picking out what they want.

Danny walks up to me.

"Those guys piss me off."

I guess he noticed me looking.

"Yeah," I say.

"They think they're so goddamn perfect."

Nolan and the other ones are loading up a big cart full with Halloween junk now. Danny returns to stocking in the back of the store so he won't have to introduce them to me. They come up to the checkout and unload paper-plates and napkins and plastic goblets and a few bags of vampire teeth and big sacks of anonymous trick-or-treat candy.

After ringing up everything, I tell Nolan the price, and he pulls out his wallet and yells back toward the back of the store, "Hey Danny! Get up here!"

The other two keep on laughing.

"What?" Danny walks up, holding onto the pricing gun. He sounds like a spoiled kid smarting off to his parents.

"You're coming to my party next week, correct?"

Nolan gives me his credit card and I run it. I wait for it to clear, thinking about how this might be the time Danny will introduce me to them. Me, his new housemate.

"Yes I'm coming to your stupid party."

One of the other guys, shiny-headed with a goatee in an Adidas t-shirt and jeans, goes, "What as?"

"Freddy."

"Freddy Krueger?"

"No." I can tell Danny is feeling me looking, feeling awkward. "Freddy Mercury."

Nolan makes a high girlish shriek. He is the perfect mix of super-polished masculinity and silly girlish flirtatiousness.

"That is fucking perfect Danny Boy."

Nolan and the other two load up the Halloween stuff.

"I'll come pick you up. You still can't drive, right?" Nolan says.

"I'll get a ride. Don't worry about it."

They take off. Danny stands up there at the checkout with me for a second.

"Nolan's an urban planner or some shit like that in city government," he says.

"He's funny," I say.

"Obnoxious as hell."

That last part is whispered. Danny looks at me then, like he is going to apologize or burst into tears or scream, but all that just goes away in one instant. He grins, and then makes a face like he is trying to kill the grin. He goes back to what he was doing, and so do I.

I take Danny to his sister's house to get his stuff after work. He's moving in with me for a little while because, as he told me, his fucking sister kicked him out. Her house is in an upscale neighborhood on a cul-de-sac, a McMansion with white brick and maroon shutters.

He comes back out a few minutes after going in, with an overstuffed duffle-bag.

"Screw them," he says, shoving the duffle-bag in the backseat.

He gets in up front, sits fuming for a second or two, and then he goes, "They are in there eating my mom's recipe lasagna. Un-fucking-believable."

I pull out. It's totally quiet in the car. I have no idea what to say. Danny, though, seems totally comfortable with being emotionally upset. It is his comfort zone, his go-to.

"Can we stop off at the liquor store?"

I have a drink with him in my one-bedroom apartment. Rum-and-Diet-Cokes for the both of us. Then he has a few more. We watch a bunch of rotten TV, ending with a repeat of a Saturday Night Live we've both seen. He told me a few days ago about the OVI and the rehab and how he can now drink because he's finally gotten it under control. He is going to crash on my couch. I keep apologizing for the couch's crappiness.

"That's basically why I'm working at Halloween City on weekends," I tell him. I'm nervous with him here, but it is a good nervousness, a welcome break from having no one in front of me here. "So I can get some new furniture. I work full-time for my dad at his flooring company, in the office there doing orders and some HR stuff."

Danny sucks down the rest of his drink, and then, "This is a beautiful couch."

He stretches out on it while I go back to my bedroom to get sheets and a pillow and blanket. By the time I get back, maybe five minutes, he's asleep and drunk-snoring. He has taken his shoes off, but that's all. He's conked out so deeply he looks like he is four years old, a giant and beautiful four-year-old. I watch him for a few moments, holding onto the pillow and sheets. Then I throw the blanket awkwardly over him. My right arm tightens up and starts to shake, reminding me, like I need to be reminded, of the cerebral palsy. The right side of my body is stiff and bent when not spazing out. As usual I ride out the spasm and then adjust the sheet and the blanket over him, Danny not even stirring. His long legs flop over the arm of the couch, almost at the knee. The snores come from deep down inside him, like a roar is trying to get out all day and it is only when he is unconscious that it can finally claw its way out into the world.

2

That next week, Friday afternoon, my dad and I go to a furniture store. I've got enough saved for a new couch, which will be my first purchase with Halloween City money. He's going to help me with the rest. I need a new kitchen table and chairs too. We go across the street from the flooring store to his friend's place, a vast warehouse of solid but cheap home furnishings.

"He'll cut us a good deal. Look here," Dad says, standing beside a big brown behemoth, a sectional.

"Won't fit."

"I'll come over and measure."

He's a tall guy with dark hair he keeps cut real short, always in polo shirts and jeans, a panicky energy about him. He can measure a whole house's floors in five minutes flat, going room to room like a tape-measuring Tasmanian devil.

I don't want him to come over to my place. He hasn't been over since Danny moved in, and I'm not telling Dad that I have a roommate, not telling my mom either. They don't feel like they have to come over and check on me anymore anyway. My mom's got a new husband and a couple of step-kids now – she's about 50 miles away, but she's always calling me. And Dad has Nancy, his girlfriend who also works in the store. I really don't think Dad would want to know. It's hard to tell, but I don't think he thinks I'll ever have a relationship, whatever that relationship might be, and if I were to just come out and tell him he'd get all nervous and frustrated and apologetic. Which I don't need.

"No," I say. "Too big."

He slumps his shoulders, his usual frantic comic gesture. We move on. Dad's friend, Rich, the owner of this place, comes out, almost his twin but with glasses and salt-and-pepper hair.

"You boys need any help?" he says.

Dad laughs, "This one here's picky."

We go through the warehouse and store and I finally choose a pretty plain but solid-looking tweed sofa, longer than the one I've got. Dad chips in on a dinette table with four chairs I like.

Rich has an anxious pitch to his voice, like he wants to get everything over with before it even starts. He calls over one of his salesmen to do the paperwork. Dad walks over with the salesman to finish his portion.

Rich says almost in a whisper to me, "He's proud of you, kiddo."

It's something Rich probably does to everyone he knows, telling them sweet little truths he thinks will make them happy. But today his saying that to me makes me happy somehow. Relieved, like I'm just like anybody else he has to deal with and say nice things to.

"Thanks," I say.

Dad and I go back to the store. I finish out the payroll for the week, making sure everybody's timecards match up with what they have signed off on. My phone goes off right when I'm logging off.

"You still cool with driving me?" Danny says. He sounds out of breath but not from running or anything, just nerves.

"Sure."

"Great. I'm getting my costume pulled together."

"Okay. I'll be home in a minute."

"Great."

I hang up and Dad's locking the front doors. Rolls and rolls of carpet and linoleum span out across the vast showroom like fallen multi-colored tree trunks.

"Who you talking to?" Dad says.

"My manager at the Halloween store. He wants me to work tonight."

I put on my coat. Dad comes over and helps get it over my arm and shoulder. Then he flicks off the rest of the back lights. The only lights left are the ones on toward the back to where we're walking.

"You are going to wear yourself out," he says, and he puts his hand on my shoulder.

"I'm fine. More money."

In the back parking-lot, Dad turns around on the way to his Navigator.

"When they deliver the furniture let me know and I'll help you get everything ready. You gonna donate your old couch to Goodwill, right?"

I nod.

"Big date tonight. Nancy and me at Red Lobster." Dad laughs. "I was going to ask you to come. But you're working now, right?"

"Yup."

I walk to my car, and Dad goes, "Be sure to eat a good dinner!"

Danny is Freddy Mercury from Live Aid, July 1985.

He's dyed his hair jet black, slicked it back, a big fake black mustache above his lip, and inside his mouth phony buck teeth. Both things he got at Halloween City. A white tank-top and a black leather bracelet on his upper left arm, a black, rhinestone-studded belt, and on his feet black and white Adidas sneakers. Tight acid-washed jeans complete the ensemble.

He's standing in my little kitchen like that, downing a rum-and-Diet-Coke.

"Nolan helped me," he says. "Design my costume."

He rolls his eyes.

"He bought it all."

"It's fucking amazing," I say.

Sometimes because of the CP my vocal cords constrict in a weird almost pinching way so my voice can sometimes sound like I'm talking through a cardboard paper-towel tube. Looking at Danny as Freddy Mercury, and me hearing myself sound like that, saying the f-word like I'm trying to be a big shot, I get a wave of embarrassment so brutally specific I want to tell him to get the fuck out of my life right then. That's the way that kind of stuff always happens. Just a sudden little spasm and then the realization blooms into a terrible crash that I'll have to survive.

Right then I want to tell Danny there's no way in hell I will be taking him to that party.

This whole last week, we got into a pretty good routine. Me and Danny usually eating Chinese takeout I'd pick up on my way home from the flooring store, and Danny telling me about his shift at Halloween City (he started working there almost full-time on Tuesday because things are picking up). We'd eat and drink rum-and-Diet-Cokes and watch Netflix shows he has always wanted to see or see again. He'd go to sleep and I would watch him go to sleep.

All I say now is, "I mean really. You look great."

Danny puts down his drink, smiling.

"Nothing really matters," he sings and his voice has a deep and lonely pitch to it, not at all Freddy-like, but still sad enough to inspire awe. At least to me.

"Anyone can see. Nothing really matters. Nothing really matters. Nothing really matters. To me."

He opens his eyes and laughs at him.

"Jesus Christ. That was shitty," he says.

I laugh and say no it was not.

Danny takes off the mustache and we eat some leftover Chinese. Yet another rum-and-Diet-Coke. He puts his mustache back on. We watch part of some serial killer doc. Then it's about 8:30 pm.

In the car, as I drive, Danny turns down the radio. I look over at him. His face is totally serious.

"I hate these parties," he says. "I really do."

He wants me to ask him why he's going. He wants to be dramatic. It's a feeling he emits, like radiation. A few nights into his stay with me Danny called his sister and she told him she was sick of his bull-shit and she wasn't going to lend him any more money, and no he can't come back to her house.

Danny said to me, right after hanging up with his sister, "That's what family is for, right? Betrayal. I took care of my mom when she was dying. Dying. OK? Dying! One whole year almost. My sister did not stop by once. Till toward the end. I had to bathe Mom. She was kind of out of her mind there for a while. And no one but me and my mom, man. Just me and her, and then it was just me and someone who used to be my mom not knowing what a goddamn light switch is, right? But I stayed there and I did what I was supposed to do because I loved my mom, you know?"

He said all that slouched on the sofa, drink in hand, his face shining out from the slouch like the flickering light of a flashlight. It was fury and self-pity and hurt, but also you could tell it was a big show he puts on. I wanted to call him on it, but then again I did not want to break the spell. Or have him leave. Because I had gotten to the point where I thought I might need him to be here.

I don't ask him anything right now. We're getting off the interstate, going toward downtown. I notice him looking at the way

I steer the wheel, using my left hand exclusively, the right just at my side. It's like he's watching me do some complicated math problem. And I think too he is wishing he was not using me this way, driving him to some party I'm not invited to.

Nolan lives in an upscale neighborhood near where they're building a new football stadium.

"Fuck it," he says. "I'm gonna have a good time. Fuck it!" He laughs. He's drunk, but just the right amount. "Thanks for taking me. I'll probably just stay over tonight and somebody can take me back to your place tomorrow in the morning."

Nolan's place is a gorgeous townhouse, old brick with white trim and shutters, an elegant front-stoop, a symbol of gentrification. It occupies a hill with a few other townhouses. All the window lights are blazing. You can see a few people inside, lots of expensive cars parked every which way.

Danny turns toward me as he opens the door.

"Thank you again," he says.

"You are welcome. See you tomorrow."

He nods. For a second though he doesn't move.

"I don't like these people," he whispers. He looks over at Nolan's house. "Why do I do this to myself?"

He laughs and then gets out and walks up and disappears into the front door.

3

I've had so many crushes I've lost count. Those are deep things, crushes. Usually I crush on guys like Danny, but then too sometimes guys just like me, with something major wrong they can't hide, and I often spin little stories about how we might hook up. How we might live together. How I might explain it all to my parents with a visual aid, as opposed to just letting them know I'm this and on top of that.

I went to a gay bar in Dayton when I turned 21 last year. Sat at a bar and got a little ripped, got some courage, went out on the dance-floor and bopped around. I actually did that. Fucking bopped around. The booze helped block out the images in the mirrored walls of this bopping around, but still I got glimpses, and even sometimes it was okay. I kind of got into the bopping. I was worn out by 10 pm though. I didn't feel defeated, just validated. No one ran from me in terror, no one bought me a drink.

In high school, I had friends, and a few I told (they were all girls), but that doesn't do anything to change the way things go. Even now I have friends at the flooring place, friends from school I still talk to and hang out with every-once-in-a-while, but nobody knows or wants to know what I want for real because it would mean I was telling them instead of getting it.

And that's that.

My phone goes off around one that morning. I'm only half-asleep, so I grab it awkwardly, fumble with the swipe.

It is Nolan's voice.

"Is this Matt?"

"Yes."

Background noises, people laughing and yelling, music.

"Danny's friend?"

"Yeah."

"He needs somebody to come and get him or we're going to have to call the fucking police."

"What?"

"Danny got shitfaced and went on a fucking rampage and now all he's screaming is call you. Call Matt."

"I'll be there in a little bit."

"Hurry. We're about five minutes from calling the cops. Not kidding. Motherfucker broke a window. He's not getting into my car."

I get there pretty quick. I stop the car and get out and walk up to the door. People are leaving, a chorus of footsteps and cars starting Nolan's inside, dressed up like some superhero I don't know the name of, but also kind of disheveled and woozy, and one of the other guys who was with at Halloween City wearing a black fright-wig, masquerading as one of the guys from KISS, the star-eyed one, and then Danny, mustache-and-buck-teeth-less now, sitting on a black leather couch in the front room. I recognize all the shit they bought on the walls and on the tables. People are getting their coats, some milling about in the kitchen. You can tell everyone is sick of Danny's bullshit. He has been the star of the show tonight.

Danny's eyes are wide open as I walk in.

Nolan turns and looks at me, and at first it's like he wants to ignore me, this anonymous little crippled guy stumbling into his home, but then it dawns on him, it's me, Matt, and I think he might be recognizing me from Halloween City.

Danny yells extravagantly, "Welcome to this magnificent party," with major emphasis on the "magnificent."

He is super stupid drunk, but the sarcasm cuts through that. His left hand is wrapped in a white dish towel, with blood seeping through.

Nolan says, "Time to go my friend."

He comes over to me, like I'm a doctor or a nurse, "He's done shit like this before, but not so bad. It's really been fun watching his decline."

The KISS guy is right beside him. He has taken off the wig, the white make-up smeared, the star around his eye melting.

"I mean we like to kid around with him, you know, and he gets all pissy and it's funny, but tonight he was just a fucking ass hole from the moment he came in."

Danny gets up, walks over to where they are talking to me, and he says to me, "Don't listen to their bullshit."

He's looks right at me. Our eyes connect because it seems like they have to. Nolan and the red-headed guy back away from him.

"I am so fucking sick of you guys judging me," Danny says. "Thinking your shit doesn't stink and treating me like I don't fucking deserve to be in your presence and then asking if you can fuck me when everybody else is not looking, or hell when everybody else is looking, well fuck you man!"

All of a sudden Danny is bawling. He bends down to me, embracing me, and I can feel the heat of his body, his wet face against my neck. I don't know what to do. I really don't. So I just go through it with him, almost unable to take on the weight but I do.

"Jesus Christ," says Nolan. "Please."

He and the KISS guy look at each other like they know the whole story before it even gets told. They just walk right into the kitchen like this never happened.

Danny does not talk in the car. He weeps. I've never really been in the presence of someone flat-out weeping. It's like sitting next to a thunderstorm. You just let it happen. You can't say anything to a thunderstorm.

I pull up outside my apartment and he gets out, and I get out. He has stopped weeping. He laughs a little.

"Fun night," he says.

I laugh too.

Inside he goes to my bedroom, like it's his room. He falls into my bed. My stomach tightens like a fist is surrounding it. I lock my door. I turn and I walk to my room.

There he is. Freddy Mercury with a busted hand and no mustache, his teeth no longer buck, lying face up, eyes open, breathing hard. It's one of those images I will never lose, that black dye seeping into his hairline like a miniature oil spill.

I go over and look at his hand. I unravel the towel. It's not bad. I go into the bathroom and get a wash cloth and some alcohol and I tell him I'm going to make sure he doesn't get infected and he just looks away. I wash the cuts, two of them, and the dried blood. I think he might need to go get stitches, but right then I can't think of anything but what's happening, how he did not fall onto the couch, how he walked in here.

Then I can see him looking at me.

"I should have invited you to that party," he whispers, looking up at the ceiling.

I lean down like I know what I'm doing. I kiss him on the mouth. He lets me do that. Then I help him get undressed. It's funny, my crappy arm, his hurt hand. He's naked, dyed black hair and suntanned chest and when I kiss his stomach I start to spaz but the spasm turns into background noise. He puts his good hand on top of my head. I can feel for a minute what it means when everything you've ever thought was not going to happen is. In those moments, it's like you're not there, you are beautifully not there, and even though it will be over real soon I know I'll return to this one time again and again in my mind, trying to feel it again in the same exact way.

4

I go in for my shift at Halloween City. Danny took Sunday off because he knew he would need to recuperate after the party. It's pretty busy all day, so my thoughts have to stay in the moment for most of the shift, but then I keep flashing on what happened and it makes me feel outside of the scene, pulled away but still doing what I need to do. There's this undercurrent of joy, like something has been figured out.

Around six, I clock off and go to the grocery store. I've only made lasagna once or twice before. My mom showed me when she was getting me ready to live on my own. She and my dad were always wanting to teach me how to make big dinners and then freeze portions so I'll always have something on hand. My mom showed me how to make chicken and noodles and pot-roast and beef stew and the list goes on, all of it portioned in little plastic containers in my freezer in the apartment.

I get hamburger and sausage and jarred marinara sauce and ricotta cheese and noodles and mozzarella to go on top.

I drive home and drag in the groceries. When I get inside the door, Danny is sitting on the couch with a blanket around him, watching another serial killer show. It's gotten dark, and he doesn't have any lights on.

I put the groceries down, after turning the kitchen light on.

"Hey," he says.

"You feeling okay?" I ask.

"Yeah. A little better."

I put on water to boil for the noodles. Turn the oven on, fry up the sausage and hamburger. I add the spices my mom told me to add. I put the noodles into boiling water.

Danny comes in and stands in the doorway.

"Lasagna," I say.

"That sounds good."

He seems devoid of any drama right then, lost without it. He goes back into the living room and watches TV. It's done in about an hour. I pull it out of the oven, my arm giving me a little trouble, but nothing unusual. I let it cool down, then plate it up. Since I don't have a kitchen table yet, we end up eating on the couch, in the TV light.

"This is pretty damn good," Danny says. His voice has a hollow kindness to it now, like he wants to disappear while he is eating what I've given him.

"Thanks."

I take a bite of what I've made, and right as I swallow someone knocks on the door, and by the sound of the knock—more of a pounding—I can tell right off who it is.

I put my plate on the floor and almost lose my balance going to answer it. It's Dad out on the cement stoop. He smiles at me, walking in, and I just back away. Danny gets up off the couch, in his underwear under the blanket, nothing else on. It's not even shock on Dad's face though, because he isn't getting it at all. He barks out a laugh, looking over at me.

"What's up?" he says to Danny.

Danny just says, "Nothing," and walks back to the bedroom to get his clothes I guess.

Dad looks over at me, and I think about what I am supposed to say, but nothing comes out of my mouth.

Dad pulls the measuring tape he uses out of his back pocket. Then he laughs, and he whispers, "Who is that?"

I tell him that it's Danny.

"Okay. Danny who?"

I bend down and pick up my plate off the floor.

"I should have called," he says. "I thought I'd make sure we could get the furniture in here okay."

I put the plate in the sink.

"Hey!" Dad says. "I'm talking to you."

He's getting mad, not knowing what else to feel, and I would tell him the whole story if it mattered, but right then I don't really have any words to work with. It feels like I've won, even though there was no contest, not even a reason to win.

Finally I just say, "He's staying with me for a little while. He's a guy I work with at Halloween City. He needed a place to stay."

Danny comes out of the bedroom, dressed in jeans and a t-shirt now. He sits down on the couch and starts putting his shoes on. Dad goes over to him.

"I think you're going to need to go," he says, almost in a whisper.

Danny nods. He looks at me as he nods.

"I mean you can't stay here sir," Dad says.

Danny gets up and laughs.

"I know that," Danny says. "Don't worry."

Danny looks at me then. I don't know what he is thinking, if he even knows what this was, what I needed it to be, but then as he goes for the door he thanks me for everything, and then he's gone.

HARD
TO
EXPLAIN

When I get there, Ruth and Dawn, Ruth's sister, are on the couch in the living room going through cardboard boxes of old Christmas decorations. Ruth is skinny, Dawn great big.

"Hey Gordo. Guess what? Your dad went off," Ruth says, getting up, pointing toward the hall.

I follow her finger and see the busted bathroom door off its hinges.

"How's it going Gordo?" Dawn asks, grunting and then getting up, putting the box of ornaments she's been going through on the floor.

Ruth hugs me before I can answer Dawn.

"A mess," she whispers into my ear.

"I'm good."

"We got Thanksgiving leftovers galore," Dawn says.

We hug, and Dawn walks back to the sofa.

"We pulled all of this Christmas stuff out of the garage out there. Thought we might put it to use," Ruth says. "You never know you're a hoarder until you have to move it all."

"Where's Trix?" I say.

Trixie, Ruth's dog, usually is barking her little head off by now.

"Sit down."

I sit down on the loveseat cattycorner to the couch, and Ruth goes into it.

"We just found out Trixie's diabetic a couple weeks back. Me and her have gotten her insulin injections down to a science where she sits in my lap in here. Your dad comes in and sees me and Trixie night before Thanksgiving, you know, doing her injection, and he just stands there looking very pissed. Verge of tears, so pissed. He's been worked up about the whole thing, me doing the injections on her. He goes, 'You love that dog more than you love me.' Then he walks into the bedroom and slams the door."

Wayne, Dawn's son, comes in. Dawn's house is two houses down, and Wayne is living with her again after his second divorce. He sits down next to the unlit fireplace, using his empty pop-can as an ashtray. A big guy with long hair and a bushy beard, he wears what he wears to work whether he's at work or not.

"You telling him everything right?" Wayne says. "It's getting bad out there. Freezing rain. Hey Gordo."

"Yes she is. Everything," Dawn says.

Wayne's smoke smell makes me want one. Ruth's face tightens up into storytelling mode again.

"So Thanksgiving morning, hell yesterday, we wake up. I slept in the spare bedroom with Trixie. Wayne you were coming over with your new gal pal around two. We wanted you to come too Gordo, but you said you had plans, right? Dawn was coming at eleven or so, to help me get it all together. Paul, he's good for the most part. He was real quiet, like he was sorry for his little Trixie outburst. We get dressed and eat our oatmeal and then I start in on peeling potatoes and all of a sudden I hear him let out a blood-curdling scream from the bathroom. I run and he's got the door locked. Trixie's in there with him, barking. I'd already checked her blood-sugar and fed her, and she was good to go. When I started in on the potatoes I forgot all about her. Well he's got her in there in the bathroom with him and he's sobbing. Just sobbing and yelling terrible stupid shit. I pound on the door and I say good God Paul what in the hell are you doing?"

Dawn says, "Lord," and Wayne lights indoor cigarette number two.

"I can hear Trixie squeak like she does when she's scared. I can hear him say he's going to kill himself. I call 911. They get here quick. He still won't open the door for the EMTs though. No window in there, no key to the lock. He starts yelling about killing himself and Trixie both so there goes the door and half the frame. They pull Paul out and I go in and get Trixie."

There's a moment where we all just look at each other, but then Wayne goes, "I'm pretty sure I can put a toilet in out there, Aunt Ruth."

"Good." Ruth turns to me. "I know your dad just got admitted but he won't be in the hospital long. He stopped taking his meds without telling me, and they'll have to regulate him but that won't be long, and then he's right back out. But this time he can't come back to the house and be around Trixie. No way, no how. I won't put her through that. She's still at the vet."

"Wow," I say.

"We're gonna turn the garage into a little apartment for him," Wayne says. "There's a waterline and a drain already for the slop-sink, so I can run lines for a stand-up shower and a toilet for him out there."

I see the outside of Ruth's red-brick ranch-style in my head, the two-car unattached garage behind the house. Ruth and her first husband had that built years ago. Her husband thought he was going to start his own engine-rebuilding business but he never did.

There's a sound coming out of the fireplace right then, almost like someone plucking on guitar strings. Then it hits us all at once. The ice. Little bits of ice coming down the chimney.

"Shit," Wayne says, standing up from the hearth there, cigarette still in his mouth. "I didn't know what the hell that was."

The night before Thanksgiving is the biggest bar night in the United States so the TGIFriday's where I used to work until recently was packed. It was 3 AM before we were done closing. Dave, my manager, came up to me while I was walking toward the office.

"Need to talk to you."

He was coming over to my place for Thanksgiving dinner that next night. We'd been fooling around since I got this job last summer. Short and stocky with a stupid little mustache he reminded me of every guy I'd ever been in love with. I was grinding my teeth a little. I'd done a couple bumps of coke to get through the shift, through everything.

"Jim called me a little while ago but I didn't have a chance to get with you it was so busy. Can't do Thanksgiving with you, man. He wants me to go with him to his sister's."

Dave widened his eyes, like what a drag, unclipping his clip-on. Jim was the older guy he lived with, a CPA with a beautiful condo in a newly developed part of town. The two of them met at some gay pride thing a couple years back. Dave licked his mouth and smiled at me and that meant I was invited to kiss him so I did, real deep, lingering there.

"No big whoop," I said after pulling away.

I walked backwards three steps or so and wished Jim and him a Happy Holiday.

"You too Gordo."

Dave drove a bright green Jeep Wrangler Sport. Jim had cosigned the loan. When I slammed into it on purpose out there in the parking lot, my head rammed into the windshield above the steering wheel. No blood but I saw stars for a second, the impact vibrating down my jaw and into my arms. I backed up and my crap car just idled there. I was stunned about how easy it was to do. The Jeep wasn't that badly damaged though. Dave came out the backdoor screaming. My car was way more messed up than his, but I was still able to take off.

"What the hell actually happened to the front end of your car Gordo?"

"I rammed into a telephone pole when it got icy."

Wayne sucks down his coffee, puts out his cigarette in the cup. We're in Ruth's kitchen this morning. The glaze the ice storm left behind a couple days ago has melted to nothing. It's like 60 degrees already.

"I might be able to fix it up for you, once I get done with your dad's place. I can at least maybe get you a tire so you can drive it to work if you get the job."

He's taking me to a job interview because the driver's side tire on my car is completely flat now.

Dave has called and texted me many times since the incident. His latest: $3000 in damage!!!! What is wrong with u?!? I'll sue your ass. You are obviously fired!!!

I go over and dump the leftover milk from my bowl of cereal into the sink. I'm in interview clothes: button-down shirt, clip-on, tan pants. Just moving forward. Wayne finished putting up the bathroom walls for Dad's place in the garage earlier this morning. It's almost a place to live now. He stands by the sink with his coffee mug and does that grin he does, like he is wanting to be everybody's best friend because he has nothing else to do except want that.

After doing what I did to Dave's Jeep, I drove directly to my apartment, and there was an eviction notice taped to my door. I hadn't paid rent for two months, spending what money I had on coke and nights out and Thanksgiving groceries. Love and self-destructiveness, at least for me, always go hand in hand. I left the notice on my door, went in and collapsed on my bed, wondering if Dave had called the cops, wondering if I had a concussion. Surprisingly no knot on my forehead, just a big red soreness.

When I woke up it was Thanksgiving. I had turned my phone off. I took a shower and ate some of the food I'd bought and watched a little TV and fell asleep and woke up that next day and did my last bump and then drove my broke-ass car in the freezing rain on a half-flat driver's side tire to Ruth's because there was nothing else I could think of to do.

The Outback Steakhouse manager is a big lady with perfect blonde hair. She interviews me in one of the back booths before they open. I gloss over my TGIF stint, focusing in on all the other restaurant jobs I'd excelled at. I am 29-years old, and restaurant work is my life, I almost say. She recognizes right off my weird desperation as something that might make me a good worker. She offers me the job after she gives me a tour.

I tell Wayne as soon as I get in his truck.

"Hell yes," says Wayne.

We drive out to a junkyard tire place he knows. He finds me a solid tire for twenty bucks. On the way back we stop off at Par's Place, this bar in a strip-mall a couple miles before Ruth and Dawn's street, near an old ramshackle golf course. Par's is where Wayne spends a lot of his time when he is not working at the warehouse or building Dad a new place to live or fixing my car.

Deanne, the bartender, says, "Wayne my man."

She's skinny with brittle red hair, smoked-out eyes, maybe around 50 or so. She hands Wayne a Coors Light automatically and still with her eyes on Wayne asks me what I want as soon as we sit down at the bar.

"Same thing."

"Plus," Wayne says. "Those wings you guys make. We are starving."

Wayne has his hair back in a ponytail. He goes to the jukebox. Deanne yells out the wings order to the guy back in the kitchen, then turns around and says to me, "And you must be Gordon, right?"

"That's me."

An old Sound Garden song comes on, a song from our youth. Wayne walks back.

"Yeah this is my sort of step-cousin," he says. "Cousin by common-law marriage. He just landed a job over there at Outback Steakhouse."

Dad and Ruth never got married because Ruth had a real bad first marriage and she swore to herself never again. My mom left Dad when I was just starting junior high. She lives in California now. Dad told me back then if I decided to go with her, that would be ok, but he'd probably end up killing himself, so I stayed. In a way, Mom leaving him allowed Dad to have something to hang his crazy on, and he somehow got better for a while. A few months after Mom leaving in fact was when he met Ruth at some VFW dance. He wasn't a veteran of any foreign war, but he had a friend who was, and he went, and there Ruth was. Meant to be. Both Ruth and Dad tell it like that.

The wings arrive and we suck them down with two more beers. Then my phone starts vibrating. I walk down to the bathroom. It's Dave telling me Jim has contacted a lawyer on his behalf. Jim in the background, that deep-pitched voice he has saying yes he contacted a really good lawyer.

"Did you hear that?" Dave says.

I hang up, turn my phone off, go back to the bar. Wayne says he needs to go out and smoke. I follow behind him, bumming a cigarette.

"Global fucking warming," Wayne says, buzzed.

Everything out here is soggy-warm and sunlit, the grass across the little road the color of old sad hair. We stand under the powerline pylon next to where he's parked his truck. The wind is strong and blowing clouds around. A bunch of geese walk through pot-hole mud-puddles like aliens trying to return to their mothership. Wayne comes up to me with his ponytail flying around behind his head. His face has a balmy contented pinkness, his eyes glittering from knowing what is about to happen. He starts to laugh under his breath, and then goes back in and pays and says goodbye to Deanne.

We use the back entrance into Dawn and Wayne's basement, the same one that we used to use as kids, through sliding-glass doors. He turns on an old living-room lamp, pushes dirty clothes off his twin-bed near the pool table. We get naked real quick, get in the bed, do what we do sometimes.

It all started when I was 13 and Wayne was 14, a few weeks after Dad and me moved in with Ruth, Dawn telling Wayne to be my friend because she felt sorry for me. It feels like we mean it more this time than any other time, though, and I kiss him like I kissed Dave, like I want him to know something from it. I remember when we first started doing it as kids, how Wayne was what I would cling to, the stuff we did together a way of separating myself from the rest of what was going on. Then one day when he was a senior in high school he got a full-time girlfriend. For a little while we stopped.

After we finish up, I put my underwear on and sit down on the bed where he is lounging on his stomach, one hand touching the floor. I almost end up telling him about the mess I'm in, but then he yawns real loud and says, "Goddamn."

"What?"

Wayne rolls over onto his back and covers himself with a sheet, his long hair out of the rubber-band, feathered out on the mattress.

"It's just funny," he says.

"It is isn't it?"

We don't say anything else.

When he gets out of Ruth's car in front of the garage, Dad looks super serious and super sad, like he's been practicing real hard for his return. I'm in Ruth's living room with Trixie now, watching through the picture-window. Dad isn't allowed in the house. He already knows that. I have Trixie's fuzzy cockapoo head right under my chin. Ruth did her blood-check before she left. Her fur smells like oatmeal and pee.

Dad is in a post-psych-unit sweat-suit and sneakers, the usual look. Ruth walks into the garage with him through the little side door.

I put Trixie down. She looks up at me for a sec and then walks over and collapses in front of the artificial Christmas tree. That thing is completely decorated with the old-timey holiday stuff they pulled out of the garage.

Wayne's at work. Dawn is over at her house, waiting on the cable guy.

I don't want to go out there right away, so I call Dave. I tell him I want to take full responsibility for what I did. Pay him in installments now that I have this new job. He says he's glad I've come around. Then he laughs.

"You little fucker."

Jim is not in the room with him obviously.

"I ended up telling Jimbo everything. He said he kind of knew from the way I acted, and how stupid it was I did what I did with you because I was your supervisor but he just said that to be bitchy you know?"

That feeling for Dave that caused me to crash into his Jeep in the first place comes back full throttle hearing his voice now. It feels good to be able to feel it in fact. To know it is still there for me to access, like any other beautiful toxic substance. I tell him I will send him the first payment next week when I get my first paycheck.

"Despite everything, you know what?" Dave says.

"What?"

"I really do kind of miss your crazy ass."

I walk over to the garage. Ruth had to show up for her shift at Urgent Care. She covers the front-desk and weighs people in. So Dad is alone. When he opens the side-door all I smell is Old Spice and fresh paint.

"Gordo."

Tall and fragile looking, salt-and-pepper hair freshly cut. They stopped off at the barbershop right after he got out I bet. I sit down on the couch they got him at Valley Thrift, and he sits down on the wingback chair Ruth found at Goodwill.

"Dad."

"Wayne did a good job in here for me."

The slow-poke voice and fidgety movements are from being re-medicated.

"What happened?" I ask.

"What?"

"You know. Trixie. Thanksgiving. The reason you're in here in your garage-apartment exile or whatever."

"I lost it."

"Really? You lost it? That's all you got?"

"I was off my meds Gordo. I felt small and crazy. It's hard to explain feeling that small and that crazy."

I look over at the little kitchen area. No stove, just a micro-wave. There are groceries on the Goodwill dinette table he has not put away yet. Cereal and a 12-pack of Diet Coke and a tube of Pringles, a loaf of bread.

"I was drinking a little too. It's embarrassing."

A big pause, and we look away from each other, both of us remembering what it takes to be together and to be happy about it, and what it takes is a total dedication to present circumstances, to pretending shit like this won't ever happen again, but knowing it certainly will.

"Ruth says you got a job at Outback over there?"

"Yup."

"You're gonna stay here with her?"

"Little while. Till I find a new place."

"I'm glad," Dad says. "We can hang out more."

I notice drool coming down his chin then. A small shiny string of it. I go get a paper-towel and give it to him and tell him he has something there.

"Oh," he says, wiping it off. "Thank you."

A few nights later we order pizza over at Dawn's house. I am off because I worked a double on Thursday at Outback. The day after Dad got back, I went to my old apartment and paid what I owed, thanks to Ruth loaning it to me. The landlord had already put all my stuff out of the apartment, in boxes and garbage bags, and I transported what I could.

Wayne is here at Ruth's with Deanne, the bartender from Par's Place. Dad is not invited because Ruth has Trixie over here with her. Plus there's beer. Dawn is in her maroon housecoat, her hair pulled back in a week-night bun. She tells us the cable guy story again, how he fixed everything, plus her bill is going to go down.

"We never watch Showtime anyway. So I just told him to take it off," she says.

Deanne is opening the four pizza boxes on the breakfast bar now. She has on jeans and a Harley Davidson t-shirt. She looks over at me like she wants to get to know me, or maybe not. Wayne is over by the kitchen sink, with the window open, smoking a cigarette.

"Hey, how's your car going?" he asks me. "Tire still good?"

"Perfect, thanks."

I am now a part of this pizza-smelling world with them.

"Come and get it you guys," Deanne says.

"Wayne and Deanne bought all of this," Dawn says proudly.

Ruth is in the den with Trixie on her lap. I go in and get a paper-plate and a couple slices. I eat both super-hot pieces way too fast, burning the fuck out of the roof of my mouth.

"Your dad is gonna be fine I think," Ruth says as she steps toward the pizza. Trixie stays out in the den, on the chair.

It's like Ruth is still trying to get used to the situation, the person she loves living in a garage she had rehabbed for him. Almost like a cage, almost like an incubator. Hell he does not seem to mind anyway. She still has her Urgent Care scrubs on. She just got off her shift a half hour or so ago.

"Yeah. I think so too," I say.

Wayne and Deanne get their pizza and go out into the den and sit on the couch to eat. Wayne puts on the basketball game. Deanne sits real close to him, and Wayne laughs because she's offering to feed him. I think about being down in the basement with him last week and when we were kids and all those other times in between. Eventually I will move on again I guess. Not too far or anything, but still I will move on like I always move on. I will find my own apartment somewhere closer to Outback. Maybe I will work my way into management. That will be my next thing. I don't know. Dave keeps calling and leaving messages, hinting around about my first payment to him, but also telling me yet again how he misses me and my crazy ass, we had something going until I lost my shit like that he says, but I have a feeling too that he almost likes what I did to his Jeep now. That it means something to him that he can't put into words.

Wayne looks over at me as Deanne feeds him a slice of pizza. We've been through this before. I know he's always here, almost like I need him to be.

"This time is different," Ruth says, almost too loud.

She gets her piece of pizza, sits down next to Dawn at the breakfast bar. TV lights give her face a shiny turquoise glamor.

"Your dad really wants to make changes in his life. You can tell. This is just what needed to happen for him to figure that out."

215

**COPYRIGHT
INFO**

True Love / original to this volume

Mars / *Christopher Street* (November 1992)

When We Go Back / *Minnesota Review* (Spring 1993 / "The Politics of AIDS" issue)

Enoch / *Christopher Street* (August 1993)

Goodbye Scott / *Christopher Street* (March 1994)

Monkeyboy Flies Through the Night / *Christopher Street* (November 1994)

Barry in the Scorched Grass / *The James White Review* (Spring 1996)

Lily of the Valley / *The James White Review* (Winter 1997)

With Gary on a Wednesday Night in Late August / *The James White Review* (Fall 1998)

Feast / Nerve.com (November 1998)

A Plant Called Eugene / *Obsessed: A Flesh and the Word Collection of Gay Erotic Memoirs* (1999)

Jamboree / Nerve.com (June 1999)

Fruitcake's First Official Murder Poem / Nerve.com (June 2000)

Traveling, Staying Still / *Nerve Magazine* (October/November 2000)

Dear Arrid Extra Dry / *Oxford Magazine* (2002)

After School / Nerve.com (August 2009)

Don't Mind if I Do / Original to this volume (2020)

Anyone Can See / Original to this volume (2020)

ABOUT THE AUTHOR

Keith Banner is the co-founder of Thunder-Sky, Inc. and Visionaries + Voices, two non-profit arts organizations in Cincinnati. He is a social worker for people with developmental disabilities full-time and taught creative writing part-time at Miami University (Oxford, Ohio) for over twenty years. He has published three works of fiction, *The Life I Lead*, a novel (Knopf, 1999), *The Smallest People Alive* (Carnegie Mellon Press, 2004), a book of short stories, and *Next to Nothing* (Lethe Press, 2014), his second collection of stories. He has published numerous short stories and essays in magazines and journals, including *American Folk Art Messenger*, *Other Voices*, *Washington Square*, *Kenyon Review*, and *Third Coast*. He received an O. Henry prize for his short story, "The Smallest People Alive," and an Ohio Arts Council individual artist fellowship for fiction. *The Smallest People Alive* was named one of the best books of the year by *Publisher's Weekly*. *Next to Nothing* was nominated for the Lambda Literary Award in 2015.

CPSIA information can be obtained
at www.ICGtesting.com
Printed in the USA
BVHW071945050520
579239BV00003B/512

9 781590 217092